Hostages of Memory

Haitham Hussein

Hostages of Memory (Novel)
Originally published as *'Rahaen Alkhateeah'*

Translated by: Jona Fras

© 2023 Dar Arab For Publishing and Translation LTD.

United Kingdom
60 Blakes Quay
Gas Works Road
RG1 3EN
Reading
United Kingdom
info@dararab.co.uk
www.dararab.co.uk

First Edition 2023
ISBN 978-1-78871-092-3

Copyrights © dararab 2023

دار عرب للنشر والترجمة
DAR ARAB FOR PUBLISHING & TRANSLATION

All rights reserved. No part of this publication may be reproduced, stored in a retrieval system or transmitted in any form or by any means, electronic, mechanical, photocopying, recording or otherwise without the prior permission of the publisher, except in the case of brief quotations embodied in reviews and other non-commercial uses permitted by copyright law.

This is a work of fiction. Unless otherwise indicated, all the names, characters, businesses, places, events and incidents in this book are either the product of the author's imagination or used in a fictitious manner. Any resemblance to actual persons, living or dead, or actual events is purely coincidental.

The views and opinions expressed in this book are those of the author(s) and do not reflect or represent the opinions of the publisher.

Text Edited: Marcia Lynx Qualey
Text Design: Nasser Al Badri
Cover Design: Hassan Almohtasib

HAITHAM HUSSEIN

HOSTAGES
of
MEMORY

A NOVEL

TRANSLATED BY JONA FRAS

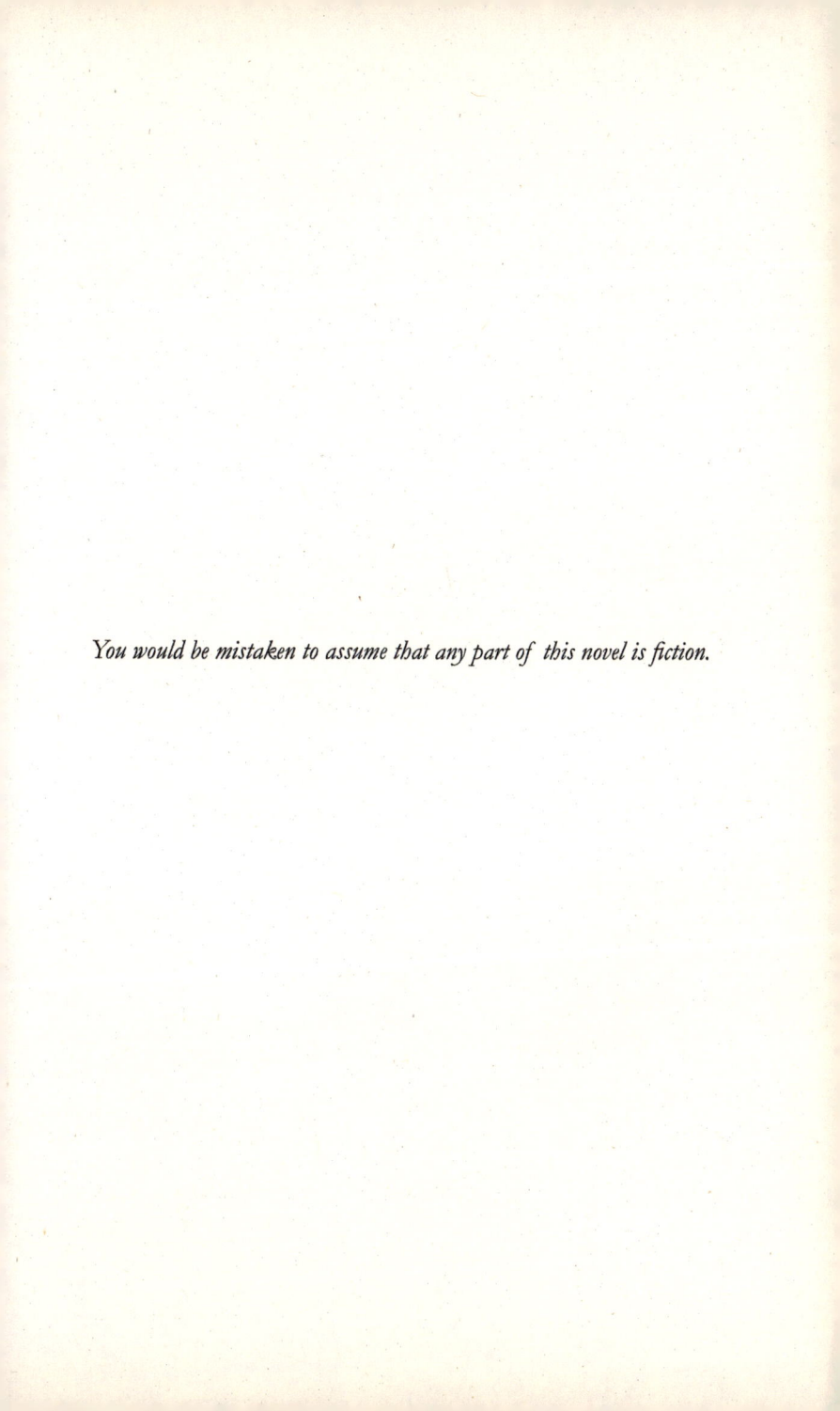

You would be mistaken to assume that any part of this novel is fiction.

Chapter 1

Shouts and cries and chants echoed in her ears. She felt a little afraid, at first, especially since she tended to stay away from crowds and large gatherings, avoiding the trap of curiosity to which so many others fell victim. There were calls from those who supported Nasser, praising him as an equal to God; others cursed him in unambiguous terms, as if he was the Devil himself risen from the depths of Hell.

She didn't understand the point of all this commotion. She did not know this Nasser who was being cursed and deified in the same moment.

And she did not feel as if she wanted to find out.

"Such bad luck that you've come here only now the Union's gone! Curse the damned conspirators. If only you'd come sooner. Surely the President would have taken care of you! Surely you would have been given assistance."

"Good for you that you haven't come here during his reign! He was a dictator. He had people conspiring with him to rob and plunder us all. He'd have stolen your goats right from under your nose! Just imagine that kind of tyranny. Not even the animals were spared."

"It was as if nature itself had conspired with him against us. Lean years and a lean Union . . . sewn together with thin thread, and even that only in his imagination."

Each and every one of them had their own personal view on the matter, and they analysed what had happened as if they'd had no role in it at all.

She heard that everything was a conspiracy. She heard everyone accuse everyone else of being a conspirator. It was as if conspiracy was some sort of disease that had infected everyone without exception. And she was very much afraid of conspiracies, plots, and schemes. She hated everything connected to them, as she knew very well what those words meant, and what they could lead to.

There were conflicting opinions, then, about the time in which Khatoune had come to town. She had not planned for anything, nor had she made any previous arrangements; it was chance alone that had driven her there. She didn't trouble herself with trying to understand what was behind all these opinions. She preferred to stay away from other people's problems. The strained, sickly mood that hung over the town had not surprised her; she had heard about the catastrophe that had befallen it a few months ago, the weight of which still lay heavy on people's chests. It left scars on their hearts that would never heal, pains that would never quite go away.

Khatoune saw, with her own eyes, the faces made pale by sorrow and suffering. She could not understand why this particular land should be singled out for so many misfortunes.

For a few days, chaos reigned in the streets. There seemed to be no end to the confusion and commotion, to hurried movements, to words ringing out in different dialects. Of these, Khatoune recognised the dialect of Mardin, though she did not understand it. Others - Egyptian, Damascene, Aleppan - she would get to know only later. Emotions flashed briefly across people's faces: laughing eyes, crying eyes, dull eyes that asked what was going on, eyes that were astonished and shocked. Eyes were messengers of the soul, points of contact and betrayal. People were wary, for the most part, in spite of the primeval chaos of outbursts of feeling. There were some who abandoned all discretion, calling for vengeance on the tyrant who had starved and impoverished them. Others went against the flow - or pretended, at least, to do so - and spouted loathing and curses for those detractors who had torn apart the threads of Arab unity.

Ancient conflicts seemed to have sprung up anew, hidden resentments that had been buried deep in people's memories. People thought they had been liberated, but they ended up plunging into new cycles of endless vengeance, trying to convince themselves with all the strength they had that the powers that reigned over their lives did not exist. Everything was happening just as it always had, and this was how it would always remain. Or so they began to say.

The disease of Unity was breaking out everywhere. It sprung from the noxious fear of having to face one's enemies alone. People's memories were still filled with stories of tragedies and disasters caused by colonialism, and they felt a burning need for someone to support them and stand by their side. Arabs, or those who had now come to be called Arabs, would cry out in utter desperation for Unity with anyone they could claim brotherhood with, wherever they lived, with little regard for geography or history. Their delusions had cheated them and clouded their minds. The popular slogans denounced and ridiculed anyone who might trouble themselves with trifles that there wouldn't be time to settle: such as rebuilding the homeland, or strengthening it, or similar kinds of nonsense. All of this paled in comparison to the greatness of the hopes and aspirations of the Arab nation.

Kurds were the same. They cried out, in private and in public, calling for Unity and the liberation of Kurdistan. They believed in hope alone, rather than the catastrophic reality around them. Many of them fell prey to grandiose ideas that, in the end, crippled them, as they were too grand for them.

Then there were the communists and the socialists - or those, at least, who had sided with them, trying to evade other kinds of duties, looking to blend into a group that would protect them and wipe out the tribal sentiments that slumbered in their hearts. Their greatest concern was the grand plan to transform human society by spreading socialism. So they had been deceived into thinking they possessed the revolutionary power to change the world, unaware that the revolution for which they were ready to risk their lives had long dispensed with its sacred ideological precepts and was ready to sell them out for the lowest possible price. It had, by now, entered its advanced stages, and its revolutionary principles had given way to retaliation and revenge.

And, as usual, there were those happy to just stand by and watch. There were pious Muslims and pious Christians, waiting to see who would float to the surface to lead them, so they could hang up his picture and praise his name. Some Arabs hid under the wing of Islam, trying to blend into society, calling out for religious brotherhood just to keep their businesses afloat. Some Christians, on the other hand, sought refuge in communism, calling out for the brotherhood of all mankind, in order to secure *their* own interests.

In the great, violent flood of changes, in the midst of its rushing waters, crossings are long and arduous. Vacant posts require occupants, whether temporary or permanent, depending on demand and in accordance with the expected result. The land was at a crossroads. It waited for someone to steer it into one direction or the other; and the feverish search had just begun.

When Khatoune arrived at the town in which she was to settle, she was happy to stay on the sidelines. The townspeople believed themselves to be the centre of the world - despite the fact that the world knew next to nothing about these people who lived on the margins of its margins. So it took days before anyone noticed her camping far out on the outskirts of town with her two little boys.

And it was not long before they got used to her presence. She remained an enigma: one which people tried to solve now and again, but which gradually retreated from view, without ever being completely forgotten. A hint of mystery was always there. "God only knows," they would say, and that settled it, outwardly at least, even if secretly they blamed Him for her presence.

Did she hold any importance at all, in that world brimming with expectation and excitement?

Should she have thought herself lucky? Or not?

At the time, she didn't pay much heed to these things. All she worried about were her children, her two boys whom she needed to take care of, and to protect from everything.

Everything.

Chapter 2

Those years were not so different from the years that had come before, nor those that followed. They were marked by all the same things, poverty and hunger and unemployment and injustice, and all as a result of tyranny and oppression. It was a natural consequence of things being run as they shouldn't have been, of nurturing failures by concealing their causes and ignoring them, under the pretext that any hindsight at all would be reactionary.

The charlatans who called for progress, who fancied themselves both its means and its end, at the same time fought desperately to keep everything as it was, for the privileged to keep their privilege, for the blind to stay blind. The intellectuals would become estranged from their own people, their spirits torn from their bodies, kept alive in a schizophrenic state that drove them to suicide - or, in the best of cases, drove them to retreat from the arena of incessant public competition. All their talk of "restoring intellectual life" was just a way to find further justifications for the crimes that were being committed, and to describe them in a different way.

In those days, cigarettes reached extortionate prices. Packets were being sold at twice their usual price; getting your hands on one was like a dream. It was an immense burden to be favoured enough to obtain one, and shopkeepers themselves needed to call in favours with the company that distributed tobacco and determined how much each was entitled to. People said that only if the seller respected you very much, and was feeling generous on top of that, would you be able to get a decent number of cigarettes - decent, in this case, meaning one whole packet, or at best two.

Butter was sold by the kilogram, since this was the portion normally allotted to each separate company and government office. The plunderers in power would usually appoint a person with the gruelling task of administrating and overseeing and giving orders. Pleasing everyone was, in general, a goal that they were not conscious of pursuing. And in the case of butter specifically, they never even really thought about it. There were ample opportunities to anger people, and in order to be held in check, their anger had to remain without a clear objective, so it would not develop into something more dangerous.

So they gave out butter in drops and trickles, like drip irrigation. Or, as the saying goes, "food for the dying." With the share to which you were entitled, you stayed on the thin line between death from starvation and famished survival. Some even described this situation as the best possible one and wrapped it up in a religious packaging, silencing everyone who had no faith in this creed whose adherents God himself had blessed.

This distribution system was a trademark discovery of tyrants - though authored, equally, by those they crushed, as an inerasable record of their submission. They were happy enough as a herd of sheep led around according to the whims of one who branded himself as being above God. One who had defied God, in fact, and sought to strip him of the holiest of his traits: his eternity.

Time passed, and things stayed much the same.

Then came the economic blockade: a time of increasing external pressures on the country, whereby external forces - that is, the world's Great Powers - exerted pressure on the regime, while the regime - that is, those who had monopolised all power in the country—exerted pressure on the people, terrorising and starving them. It bombarded them with extravagant rhetoric that demonised anyone who doubted its credibility. It disproved the laws of physics, which stated that high pressure eventually leads to an explosion: reality demonstrated, as it continues to demonstrate today, that pressure generates only desolation and acquiescence.

It may be that the sheer potency of that kind of pressure, when applied, transcends scientific principles. Those who plunder and oppress their people do not always see their deeds held to account; these claim to be inspired by the Almighty. Upon assuming power, did the Caliph al-Mutawakkil not gather around himself dozens of scholars that certified and swore to him that he would not be held to account on Judgment Day? And this a caliph of cowards and capitulators! Today, any self-respecting contemporary tyrant, upon assuming his reign of tyranny, also has it sworn to him that he will not be judged. He reigns by God's order. Nobody else's. And even if a follower is pushed far enough by their fear to find the courage, they are either a conspirator, or ignorant, or have some other secret agenda, or are simply deranged and don't know what they're talking about - in which case they are, of course, not to be blamed for their actions, just like any other person of unsound mind. Once the obedient worshippers realise this, and if they wish to acquit themselves from the charges of conspiracy or ignorance or secret agendas, they must either allege they were duped or seek refuge in madness. Anyone who risks suicide in this way, driven by fear transformed into boldness, knows that they have "lost it", as people say - meaning that they've lost all heed for the value of their life, and live on happy in their insanity, in the midst of miserable cowards paralysed by fear, whipped into submission by their transgressions.

A people viewed and treated as a herd of sheep: deceived by charlatans from among their own number, who worked through them like a cancerous growth, without mercy of indulgence, misled by the propaganda of steadfastness and engagement. Steadfastness, yes, in the face of the needs of the people - or rather the "flock", an appealing word for them as it reminded them of the word "shepherd," in addition to its religious connotations, which reinforced its meaning and disguised some of the malice behind it. And engagement - engagement, that is, with the desires and hopes of the people, so they would not rebel against their caretakers. For all the struggles they had fought, these people would never reach the point at which they could be let out of their diapers; they needed to be taken care of, herded and led by the noble-minded among them. They needed to be treated gently, armed and armoured against the claws of foreign oppression that disguised themselves perniciously as the people's demands - "demands" which, of course, had no rightful basis in law.

The strong exterminated the weak: they pushed, and they always pushed down. The process ended with the extermination of the people, shattering their hopes, rooting out their desires. Those pushing down agreed to leave the ones at the bottom to those further below them, at the expense of those a little further up. Those who perished were born to perish, and nothing else. So said the cowards hiding in their little glass houses, where their nakedness was fully visible, with nothing to hide the disgrace they sought to inflict on the people.

This world of pressures and counter-pressures of various sorts, full of hoarding and plundering and exploitation, where everyone was constantly looking out for their own benefit: this was the world in which Grandma Khatoune's sons grew up. The two Sufis, as they were known: Ali and Ahmad, or Alo and Ahme, as people called them. Later, they also came to be called the Bifazo. This was the name by which they became famous, and through which they were forever described and defined.

Chapter 3

Grandma Khatoune would break stale bread into pieces and put these pieces into canvas bags to sell. This was how she reminded herself of her past life, when she wandered from village to village in the lands known as Jayaye Omriyan. There wasn't a single village she had not visited, and while she did come to know quite a few people in each of them, she never seemed to be able to settle down. She was always on the move, as if there were a crime pursuing her that she never could quite flee from, or a sin for which she had not received forgiveness. She did, finally, come to settle in Amouda, where she contented herself with a hut on the outskirts of town. Her children stayed with her, two small boys, and a black goat that was never tied up and, during the night, slept with them in the hut.

She was cautious toward everyone at the beginning. Whenever someone approached her house, she would draw back, asking them sharply after their business before they could step closer. Gradually, once she had reassured herself that the locals only wanted to learn her story, do her a favour or two, perhaps discover some distant relation of hers - she came to trust them a little more. But she did not throw herself blindly into their graces. She ignored most of their offers, and she would shut down any talk regarding the place she had come from, or her family or relatives. "From the wide lands of God," was all she would say. Sometimes, she'd be a little more specific, although only by repeating something everyone already knew: that she was from "above the border." And that, really, was the end of it.

People came to accept this and would no longer ask her about it -

except occasionally. So she came to be known as Khatoune of Jayaye.

She experienced her share of calamity and misfortune during her first twenty-five years in the town. She would sew bedcovers and raise cows to provide for her little family. She also worked as a midwife, and she didn't much care about what she would sometimes hear from this or that woman whom she'd helped deliver: that she was heartless, that she was never stirred by their screams or cries for help during labour - as if they were trying to imply that she had not delivered her two sons herself, or had never experienced the iron-melting pains of childbirth. She would say only that it was her duty to do as she did, for the new mothers' sake. Labour wasn't a time to show empathy; it would only cause harm.

Her sons grew up working as delivery boys in the market. They both wore woollen skullcaps and prayed dutifully at the mosque every Friday. People came to like them, and, as the years passed, they would no longer ask them about why they'd come to Amouda, or any other of Grandma Khatoune's many secrets - which, it seemed, would take to her grave, never relieving her soul of the pain of suppressing them. She would not reveal them to anyone, not even her boys, no matter how much they begged her to do so. She never told them anything more than what she told everyone else. So they were forced to accept her silence, and—like everyone else - stopped asking. Still, it troubled them, from time to time.

Sufi Alo reached and passed thirty without once broaching the subject of marriage with his mother, or, for that matter, his brother. He knew very well how pitiful their circumstances were, even as he and his brother advanced from delivery boys to street peddlers to partners in a small store in the Arsah Market. But then came the day when Sufi Farho told Alo to wait for him at the gate of the mosque after evening prayers, and asked him to marry his daughter.

The women called this daughter of Farho's Shekrawka Karrik, meaning she was nearly deaf. Sufi Farho's offer to Sufi Alo came on the basis of their shared religious devotion, and because Alo had proven his good nature and excellent morals, and also because Alo was a capable worker and Farho wouldn't have to worry about his daughter if she was married to him. He hastened to add that he would, of course, help Alo cover some of the wedding expenses. He wouldn't ask for a bride-price either; if Alo upheld his promise to take care of his daughter, that was bride-price enough.

Alo was more than a little stunned, and he accepted Farho's offer there and then. He swore he would never take his eyes off Farho's daughter, and never make her want for anything. He did not care if his betrothed was old or deaf, or that Sufi Farho may have approached him as a last resort for a daughter whose hand had never been asked for, and who had lost all hope of marrying. For Alo, to become a son-in-law to someone like Farho had never been more than a distant dream. Yet here he was now, on the verge of this dream becoming reality .

They both had supernatural explanations ready to account for their good fortune. Alo liked to think it was God's own unadulterated love that chose him from among so many others. Farho outwardly ascribed it to fate, while he kept to himself the true reasons that had forced him to make his proposal.

But the new groom did not care to look for these reasons, and neither did Grandma Khatoune. The marriage was the right way forward. This they knew, or at least convinced themselves they did.

Chapter 4

After Sufi Farho had made Alo jump with joy over tidings he'd never dared to dream of hearing, he added one further remark. Just a small one, he said, but he was obliged to mention it. His daughter had a "hearing problem."

Alo didn't quite know how to respond to Sufi Farho's overflowing generosity, and his sincerity embarrassed him. He had little to say other than that of course he did not attach any sort of importance to the issue of hearing problems. And so it was—even later on, when the "hearing problem" turned out to be near-complete deafness, one with where no amount of shouting did any good. You had to use hand gestures, or yell loudly enough that all the neighbours would hear. But Alo was happy to live a quiet life, without all the likely annoyances his wife might have brought him with gossip and prattling.

And so was she. Her deafness, and her father's cruelty, had imposed a total silence upon her life. She lived isolated from everything, her world confined to the demands of housework and motherhood. As for her conjugal duties, they soon virtually disappeared; she got used to ignoring and suppressing her own desires, like most other women she knew, and only responded to those of her husband, even as these grew less and less frequent as time went on.

She'd lost her hearing more than twenty years before, when she was still a child. She was sweeping the front stoop on a summer evening, a little before sunset. She had splashed a bit of water on the floor so she wouldn't raise dust when she suddenly caught sight of her father, marching swiftly home, returning early from the market. Farho was shouting and cursing at her, and when he came near, he punched her so hard she fell, hitting her head on the wall behind her. He then ordered her to get inside the house, with another stream of curses, and swore by God that he would murder her if he saw her sweeping the front stoop ever again.

Another story lay behind this monstrous behaviour of Sufi Farho's, which can be told here in brief. When he was in the market that day after the afternoon prayers, he happened to overhear a conversation among a group of delivery boys - whom he would later describe as filthy and depraved - as they sipped their tea and exchanged whispered remarks about the wiles of women.

These were men well-versed in sowing mistrust and spinning tales that revealed people to be malicious and wicked, even if they appeared innocent. A girl might, for example, use the excuse of sweeping the front stoop in order to go outside at a particular time she'd agreed on with her lover. She would take her time sweeping and standing around until her lover came by and saw her or spoke to her so that they could arrange another meeting; and this would, later on, lead to disaster and tragedy, when the lovers met somewhere far from the eyes of the people, and the man would take what he wanted from her and then cast her aside like a wet rag .

Before Sufi Farho could fully absorb the implications of what he had just heard, another of the delivery boys interjected that one should get rid of such a girl immediately by marrying her off as soon as the "sieve passes between her legs," that is, as soon as she matured. "Wean her off the tit and find her something harder to suck on," he added, to general laughter.

These warnings echoed in Farho Tawtus' ears, and doubt began to creep over him. He hadn't been able to find a match for his daughter, and so, slowly, his suspicions grew. They're right, he told himself. They have to be.

He rushed home for sunset prayer, aching to empty his bladder but forced to wait unless he wanted to invalidate the ablutions he'd taken such pains to perform earlier that day. When he spotted his daughter sweeping the house's front stoop without a veil on, he at once remembered what the delivery boys had been saying. Rage and jealousy overcame him, and so he did what he did. While his daughter still considered herself a child, her father and everyone else regarded girls of her age as women, with honour that had to be protected. So she became a victim of her own naïve good opinion of herself—or rather, the mistrust of her father. She was seen as an adult, and on this basis, she was judged.

This incident saved her, at least, from what others might have had to say about her. Farho, however, would never again be at peace, and would never stop asking God's forgiveness for his suspicions about his daughter. He tried to atone for his actions by spoiling her, by being kind to her, by speaking to her gently and sparing her work and generally asking less from her. And yet she was punished if she spoke up, and she was left in pain if she remained silent. She was only ever happy when she was doing housework. She remained scrupulous and reliable in all she did, and she kept her honour intact.

But Farho's punch had already tainted her inexorably. Suspicions swirled around her, as did malicious gossip, which cared only about what it wanted to find, no matter how convincing other answers might have been. Farho chastised himself over and over for using violence when he shouldn't have. Still, his madness and rashness and blind jealousy had kindled the fire, and no amount of remorse on his part could put it out. The genie of speculation and slander was out of its bottle; and, as the proverb says, vicious tongues aren't a belt one can tighten or loosen whenever one wants.

Chapter 5

Grandma Khatoune gave her blessing to the marriage. She knew Farho's daughter to be honest and kind-hearted, and also that she excelled in her knowledge of the Qur'an, a project of her father's, who had himself been deprived of the benefits of literacy. As had Alo, in fact. They knew their numbers and accounts, gained through work and travel, and that was all. Farho had tried to compensate for his lack of education through his daughter, while Alo, for his part, subsequently found her talents to be good cover for his weaknesses.

The little house was now to be split in two: one part for the bride and groom, and another for Ahme and his mother. Alo was given the big room, as they called it - though it was big only by the standards of their household, as it was barely five metres across. The other room, even smaller, from then on belonged to Grandma Khatoune and Ahme.

The rest stayed as it was: a small kitchen with a stone-paved corner used for washing, and the toilet, which was an open cabin at the edge of the courtyard. Its walls came up to less than a metre and a half, so you could see the head and shoulders of whoever was inside before they'd sat down. Sometimes, if the person was particularly tall, the head jutted over even while they were seated. Inside, there was a hole in the ground, with some stones lain around to give the impression of a toilet. It wouldn't do, in any case, for there to be a house without one - even though neither Alo nor Ahme entered it more than once or twice a month. They preferred to relieve themselves in the open, in the field behind the house.

They would take their jug of water with them and light a cigarette while they did their business. It was just one more little ritual that gave them pleasure and a small feeling of freedom. Sometimes, when life weighed particularly heavily upon them, they would head for the public toilets at the mosque. Though they would be quite upset to hear, as people said from time to time, that the mosque was a place meant for worship rather than taking care of your bodily needs, they visited it for prayer much more often than they did to merely use the facilities.

On a day-to-day basis, things went on much as they had before. The household's needs also stayed much the sam - though only until Farho's daughter gave birth to her first child, a girl. Alo chose to name her Khatoune, after his mother: to keep her memory alive, as it was said. But the girl was born prematurely and quickly passed away, consumed by an attack of measles that her little body was too fragile to withstand, on top of other ailments and weaknesses she had inherited from her parents.

Alo was secretly glad of this, though he never found the courage to express it out loud, as such sentiments were forbidden by his faith. But even though it was what God had decided, he had never asked for it. His life so far had brought him only poverty and helplessness, and since girls were a burden "until their deathbed," as it was said, it was a care too heavy for him to take on.

So he hid how he felt, and put on a guise of mourning for a few days, as was appropriate for a father who had lost a daughter, or someone else dear to him. His secret joy only grew further, though, once he heard that those fathers whose children die young go straight into Heaven, as a reward for their forbearance. Such children would enter Heaven only once their fathers and mothers had already done so, and then they would turn into little birds that fluttered over their parents' heads.

His daughter's death thus secured Alo a good place in the next world, saved him money in this one, and won him sympathy from all those around him. A profitable bargain, then, by any reckoning.

A year and a few months later, Shekrawka gave birth to a boy. This child became the family's greatest joy and treasure: he ensured the continuation of their line—however obscure it was—and Alo set much of his hopes on him regarding their future. He entrusted the duty of naming the boy to their neighbour, the town teacher, and even swore an oath to that effect. "Teacher and no other!"

While Teacher did not visit the mosque often, let alone follow a sheikh or belong to a Sufi order, his conduct was exemplary, and his good manners were praised by all. Alo did not know him very well, but this only increased his awe and respect for the man; he believed Teacher to be doing noble work, as he not only educated the children of Amouda, but also helped those in need, and never withheld his advice if someone asked for it.

Alo was, therefore, quite confident that Teacher would choose a name from the list of those that were religiously agreeable. But in this, Teacher disappointed him. He suggested, instead, the name Hawar, which he said was very beautiful, and most appropriate.

"I hope for him to be a true embodiment of his name," Teacher added. "A cry of rejection for all that his ancestors have suffered! It will light the fire of revolution against those who turned his family into vagabonds and beggars, and made of him a refugee in every place he will run to."

Teacher's eyes were fixed on the horizon as he said this, his words driven by unfathomable hopes. Alo, who really didn't understand much of what this man was on about, was hesitant to use the name, but he was equally unable to go back on his oath. In the end, he settled for what had been ordained for hi - hoping that, one day, his son would become an educated man, and not have to repeat the course of his father's wretched life, as a delivery boy weighed down by the loads on his shoulders, or a street peddler whose hands grew sore from pushing his cart, his voice raw and hoarse from calling out to passers-by.

Chapter 6

Sufi Alo and Sufi Ahme were brothers, but in their early thirties, everyone who know them said they were like twins. Ahme treated Alo as his equal and closest friend. They were business partners for many years, having started work together as delivery boys, then street peddlers. They shared a single cart between them: one of them would cry out while the other pushed, and then they would switch. After they had worked some years as peddlers and saved a bit of money, they were able to rent a shop in the Arsah Market. This became their little kingdom, where they were happy, and where they finally found their independence.

They never argued. They agreed on everything. They had complete, unspoken trust in each other, and it never occurred to either Sufi that it could be otherwise. They were much the same in character, although their interactions were mostly concerned with the business of buying and selling, and they did not discuss much beyond that, as long as life kept to its peaceful and carefree routine.

They shared their friendships and acquaintances, all of which were confined to the marketplace. It didn't make much of a difference if it was one or the other, though some clients did prefer to buy when Ahme was present, as he was more flexible in his dealings and would sometimes give a better price to those who needed it, as if wanting to give charity for the souls of his dead ancestors, about whom he knew nothing.

When they were in the shop together, it wouldn't matter who was sitting in the shopkeeper's chair behind the wooden desk - a desk which they had made together, by gathering pieces of wood and assembling them. The one sitting in the shopkeeper's chair would be the one with the money purse at his belt, divided in two: one side for paper money, the other for coins. Alo was the one doing it in the mornings; Ahme did it in the evenings, in exactly the same way.

So it became known in the market that whoever had the money purse on his belt was the one in charge. They had kept to this tradition ever since they first began to work as peddlers, even after they had left the cart behind and settled down in the shop. They grew well accustomed to checking that their money was safe in the purse, even if it was always closed and they had the key with them. They loved to move the coins around and hear them rattle; or, whenever they found themselves with nothing else to do, they would count the paper notes one by one, arranging them according to size and removing the tattered ones, which they would give back as change to their customers. Those notes that looked nice and fresh - as if they'd just been taken out of the bank, as they liked to say - those, they would wave around like little flags, to make a sweet, crisp, rustling sound.

"Sweeter than the shuffling feet of the virgins in Heaven!"

So Alo said to Ahme. When Ahme smiled at this description, Alo laughed, and added:

"Oh, if only we had a machine that could print money! I'd leave it running fifty hours a day."

So it went whenever they were alone. Their work was never-ending, although usually they had some time to themselves after afternoon prayer, when the market was nearly empty apart from the shopkeepers and the peddlers with their carts. Groups of different sizes gathered for discussions around pots of tea; this was "hunting time", as they said in the market, because the remaining goods were considered a source of possible profit, however pitiful the price for which they ended up being sold. Old merchandise would lose a lot of its value, and you could either give it to charity or throw it out.

The Sufis would smoke tobacco from the same tin, but they would never share a cigarette. They could hardly enjoy it unless they kept it for themselves, and neither of them would blame the other for it.

Like any skilled traders, they spent much of their time discussing the issues of their business. They analysed the market, weighed whether to sell certain goods or not based on demand, then came up with a plan that they carried out in the following few days. So it was that Alo came up with the idea of buying up a huge amount of onions. He realised that the amount planted would not satisfy the increasing demand, and imports had all but stopped. It was their chance to strike! Ahme was sceptical at first, but his brother's detailed analysis slowly won him over. He didn't like taking risks; what pleased him most about their business was that they did not deal with debt and its associated headaches. "If you can't afford fruit and vegetables, you'll have to eat soup or bulghur wheat instead." That was what they told themselves, over and over, and they kept to it. They were more than happy to take fruit or vegetables that were already past their best, or had dried out in storage and barely looked like anything, and that no longer seemed profitable.

They started to buy up the onions - in secret, as traders were a jealous lot. They stored them in one place and covered them in plastic and canvas bags for protection. Soon enough, they accumulated a huge quantity of onions, until they all but disappeared from the market. The once-doubtful Ahme began to get excited.

"Let's sell them now!" he whispered to his brother. "We've bought them all up, at a really low price, and now they'll give us double that for it! It's our chance, Alo! A once-in-a-lifetime chance. We have to do it!"

Alo paid him little heed; he was too busy laughing inside, thinking of the huge profits that they would realise, that would make them rich for the rest of their lives, all but compensating for their days of toil as delivery boys in the town's dusty streets.

"Relax, Ahme. Good things come to those who wait!"

He spoke calmly, rolling a cigarette for himself and another for Ahme. When one of their neighbours passed in front of their shop, he called out to him, and rolled him a cigarette too; for he saw himself as rich, and generous, and hospitable. He could hardly hide his delight; it made him forget all the toil that he had suffered. After all, they would be very rich, and in just a few days' time.

"Be patient," he told Ahme. "Just be patient, my brother. Most of the job is done, and there's not much time left. God knows we'll live like kings in a few days. Be patient."

Still, Ahme was nervous. He fidgeted constantly, and he couldn't sit in one place for long. He feared that something would happen that they had somehow overlooked. The thought that the onions might be stolen made him restless; they were, after all, in peak demand at the market—and he and his brother were stockpiling them. He was even more worried when he heard at the mosque, one day at afternoon prayer, that those who hoarded goods were a menace to society, as they prevented believers from obtaining the profits and blessings that were due to them from Almighty God.

When Ahme shared with Alo his fears of the torment that may yet await them in the afterlife, his brother sought to comfort him.

"There is nothing impious about business! The Glorious Prophet himself worked in trade and knew all its secrets, and how it involves both profit and loss. So here we are, Ahme, with the deal of our lives in front of us. And we will lose nothing!"

"If God wills it, Alo. If God wills it!"

"Oh, come on! Yes, if God wills it, a thousand times. Are you happy now, my Sufi?"

"Alo!" Ahme looked shocked. "What's this now? Are you trying to make light of God's name? God save me from you and your foolishness. You've become a father, and you still act like you're a child! If you don't care about yourself, at least think of your son...." Ahme raised his finger high. "In God's name, I swear I have nothing to do with this foolishness. And may I never have a share in any profit that does not come by the grace of Almighty God!" He wiped his hand on his face, as if he had just recited the fatiha, then turned back to his brother. "You've become arrogant, Alo! Great wealth is within your grasp, and you lose your faith in God. Is this the Sufi that I know? It's like I barely know you anymore! Doubting God's will might sour your words, and you jeopardise your soul over the money that you don't even have yet."

"Well!" Alo said. "God is generous, Ahme, and forgiving. I swear to you, you're overreacting. I didn't mean anything like that at all! It's you putting words in my mouth. You're just worried about the merchandise, and about the risks, and so you're exaggerating." He smiled to lighten the mood a little. "Your cowardice, Ahme, that's what will ruin us. God may not forgive you again if you mistrust your brother! See, these are the differences slowly coming between us, to fracture our brotherly love, our only strength in our short earthly lives." And as if to absolve himself, he added, "I see now that we have become enemies, and before we could ever become rich! Yet how could we become rich together, when surely you will renounce me, with some excuse or other."

"Really?" Ahme said, startled. "Really, Alo? Well, now it's you putting words in my mouth! Don't try to blame me for this mess!"

He tossed down his cigarette and crushed it with his foot, and then ground it down with a circular motion, until barely a trace of the butt remained. It was as if Ahme were trying to take revenge on his brother for accusing him of such horrible thoughts, of which he was entirely innocent. What rankled most was that his kindness and reliability were being questioned.

Alo saw all these thoughts cross his brother's face. "I can see now, Ahmad, how angry you are," he said, in a conciliatory tone. "Pray for the Prophet and trust in God's mercy. Come, sit down with me." He pushed aside some empty boxes and gestured his brother to sit.

Ahme forgave him, then, especially when he heard him say his full name. Ahmad. It reminded him of those most dear to him, and his kindest and sweetest memories. Nobody called him by his birth name, other than the three people he loved most in his life: his mother; the sheikh, who would always refer to him as Ahmad, even in his absence, and certainly whenever he asked him to do something; and his brother, in their most difficult moments together, when they were at their closest and needed each other most. When Ahme was fuming with rage, then that name, said in a kind, loving voice, would quiet the worries that were gnawing at him, calm him down and reassure him. It would convince him that his brother could not do anything that was not good for them.

Everyone else just called him Ahme; he was not annoyed by this, and often forgot his real name was Ahmad at all. Once, when he was waiting in a crowd outside the government building for his turn at food rations, the official was calling out people's first and last names. When his name was called - his birth name, as it was written on his ID - Ahme didn't recognise it, and he didn't answer. The official repeated his name a few more times, to no avail; and only when he started cursing the idiot who wouldn't take his turn promptly, and was stupid enough to run off with the kids and donkeys in the streets, did Ahme realise that it was his name that was being called. He was Ahmad! His shock at this, however, could not outweigh the disaster of having missed his turn, as it couldn't save him from the official's mocking comments - to which Ahme didn't respond, given that the official could postpone his turn indefinitely, or even cross him off the list for being too late.

"God will provide for you yet," the official told him, after the food had finally run out. "Next time, when your turn comes, it will be under Ahme. But you have to change your name on the ID!"

Ahme got through this embarrassment, more or less, because he trusted God would make everything right. He would comfort himself, as many did, that as long as people were uncaring, insensitive, and tried to strip themselves of all true links to others, there was no reason for him to get involved in something bigger than himself, to get lost in it and take the blame.

But in doing so, he got lost nonetheless. He was humiliated and stripped of his humanity, yet still he invented excuses, trying to ignore the insult he had suffered, and the chuckles and laughter directed at him for forgetting his name. He wanted to shout in the official's face for giving himself and the stupid crowd a lively interlude at Ahme's expense. They sank their fangs into him, and they emptied all their poison and hatred into him. They expressed their hatred for injustice and tyranny by taking it out on another poor soul. Much like the folk proverb: "All that a bird suffers, it does to its young."

"The virgins of Heaven have enchanted you, oh Sufi!" the official went on. "They stole your manhood and captured your soul! I fear that Azrael himself won't be able to find you, when he comes for you. He'll be looking for Ahmad, and he won't find him! You've found a way to cheat death, my man! Isn't that so, Ahmadji, you little fart!"

If Alo had been in Ahme's place, he might have shouted back:

"Your mother drove me crazy, your wife drank my semen, and your sister fucked a donkey. Plus your daughter did it with the kids from the street!"

Or perhaps he would have just muttered it under his breath.

While these bittersweet memories were coming back to him, Ahme stuck his little finger into his ear, pushing it around slowly to clear out the earwax. He took out his finger and inspected the dirty yellow lump that he had just extracted, mixed up with a bit of foam that had dried in there when he had last washed. It looked a bit like a dried-up swamp. It made him happy: he saw in that dirty lump the crowd that had mocked him. He thought about where he could put it; he searched his pocket for the piece of cloth he usually carried with him, but he couldn't find it. Without really thinking about it, he realised that sticking the lump in his pocket would be the best thing to do: his trousers were dark, and a little bit of dirt on them wouldn't show.

He straightened in his seat and felt the comfort of his balls settling down in their sack. Well, he thought, praise be to God.

"Oh, Ahmad. I swear to God, brother, I didn't mean to upset you with what I said. You're so irritable these days! Come on, now. Let's go to the mosque, let's do the ablutions, and seek refuge from Satan and ask God's forgiveness."

Ahme suddenly remembered the stale breadcrumbs that he would keep in his pocket whenever he would make his pilgrimage to the sheikh's house. He liked to nibble on them whenever he felt irritable or annoyed with something. They were like a sedative of sorts, calming him down and stilling his heartbeat, and settling the commotion in his soul. They would imbue him with the generosity that he so desperately needed. He wished that his brother would believe him and take his advice, taking a crumb of bread to make his worries go away, to calm his spirit and his nerves. It was the best possible medicine, the cure a healer would give his beloved, for this was blessed bread. He asked Alo to do the same. Before, Ahme would give these crumbs to whoever he met or whoever bought anything from him. But when his pilgrimages had grown infrequent due to his preoccupation with the filth of earthly life, as he might say, he grew jealous of his breadcrumbs, and would no longer give them out to all and sundry but rather hid them away for those he cared about, as they would need them at times of grief and misfortune. They were a magic formula that possessed hidden medicinal properties: it could cure many diseases and prevented you from contracting others. Their effects were nearly instantaneous, as if they were a command from God who imprinted his will onto the void and sealed it with the eternal seal of his omniscience.

Ahme knew that his brother wasn't trying to dismiss his concerns;

and yet, he also saw that the wound would take time to heal. Until then, their relationship wouldn't quite be the same.

He wished so much, then, that his brother would believe him, the way he used to, and give him some brotherly advice. He swore on their brotherly honour, both sacred and profane, that he didn't wish anything for them that could be considered forbidden, and that he would not be content if it was otherwise. But his worries grew when Alo flung an arm out to stop him; he waved left and right, then made as if to close his eyes and sew up his lips, as if to forbid him from disclosing his plans.

Chapter 7

Ahme felt his faith in God begin to weaken when he noticed, as happened more than once, that he would be distracted during prayer, and would no longer know how many movements he had already done and would then have to repeat the whole prayer from the start. He chastised himself a lot over this, beginning to doubt the strength and resilience of his relationship with his Lord God. He complained of these problems to his sheikh, divulging his suffering in a small, soft voice, tears sparkling in his eyes. The sheikh was accompanied by one of his disciples, a certain Faqqih Abd al-Wahhab, who was quick to reprove him:

"You are sinful, Sufi Ahme! You know that very well."

With that, Faqqih was of course referring to Ahme's stockpiling of onions with his brother Alo. He quickly realised that he might have overreached, and that he perhaps should not have given his judgment without first asking permission from his sheikh. But the sheikh did not seem to mind; he pondered for a time, then resorted to his usual strategy of persuasion, which was to tell a story of the Prophet and his companions, or one of the four imams, such as the Imam Shafi'i. He faced Faqqih and Ahme both, but without looking either of them in the eye. They did not catch his gaze either, as they would always keep their heads bent low in his presence.

"Absent-mindedness, my son, is inevitable," the sheikh began. "Praise be to God who said, 'Woe be upon those who are distracted from their prayers.' But he did not say, 'Woe be upon those who are distracted during their prayers.' There is a hadith that goes as follows: A man came to the Prophet, God's prayers and peace be upon him, and he said to him: 'Oh Prophet of God, I get distracted during prayer.' Ali, may God bless him, was sitting there, and he rebuked the man, and said that distraction during prayer was a most loathful thing. Then the Prophet, God's prayers and peace be upon him, said: 'Rise, Ali, and pray; and I will give you my cloak.' And when Ali prayed, he was distracted, and he got confused and did not know which cloak the Prophet would give him. When he finished his prayer, he admitted that he was distracted during it, and he spoke more kindly to the questioner. And it was a lesson for all."

"And so," Faqqih cut in, "you might be distracted and think about worldly matters, without paying attention to what you are reading or saying. And that means that Satan is whispering evil into your heart and trying to distract you from your prayer."

"And as for sinfulness," the sheikh went on, "that also is part of human nature. You must overcome it, as much as is possible, by worshipping God, and invoking his name, and praising him, and thanking him, in all that happens. See, the Imam Shafi'i was one of those people who could memorise a page just by looking at it. But his ability to do so was weaker on certain days than others. So the Imam complained to his sheikh, and he tells us about it in a poem:

I complained to Waki' about my poor memory;

he advised me to abandon sin.

And he said: Indeed, knowing God is light;

and the light of God is not granted to a sinner.

"And do you know what his sin was? I'll tell you! He had been walking around praising God when he noticed, without wanting to, the ankle of a girl. And he was most troubled because he had sinned like this, and he was preoccupied and exhausted by it. So here we are, we who are weak in faith, and who are the most sinful of God's creatures, yet we must be the best possible sinners, repent to God for every sin, and make our hearts pure. We must wish the best for all the Muslims, until God blesses us, according to our will and love, with good and happiness for all."

The sheikh then directed some final words to Ahme. "Do not worry, Ahmad, my son." Hearing him say his name, his birth name, cheered Ahme greatly and calmed his soul. "Do not worry," the sheikh went on, "and do not be afraid. Repent to God, and persist in your prayers to Him, and ask Him for forgiveness; for He is the Acceptor of Repentance. And, if He wills it, He will forgive your sins. You should say to yourself out loud, before every prayer: 'Oh God, bless the day when we stand before You in judgment, and disgrace us not.' Then you should spit to your left three times and say: 'I seek refuge with God from the accursed Satan.'"

Ahmad left much reassured, as he usually did from meetings with his sheikh. His soul was filled with the kind of bliss that he had been craving for a while, and which he'd thought he would never find again. He resolved to avoid everything that could distract him from worshipping God and praising His name - whatever that would be. Belief must come with worship of God the Creator. He already had much; and wanting to enrich yourself, or the lust for money without charity, meant straying from the true path of God.

Sufi Ahme rushed to the storeroom, took a sack of onions, and carried it back to his sheikh's house. He asked the sheikh to let him know when he ran out, so he could bring him more.

Chapter 8

The Sufis bought up and stored all the onions they could get their hands on. They bought all the onions from the neighbouring farms, and also those that were supposed to go the market in Qamishli. Their cunning plan was supposed to change their lives forever, to provide them with what had been denied them, and to give them all that they might ever want.

Or so they thought.

They were so deeply absorbed in their buying and stockpiling that they never noticed the rotting stench that had come to attract all the flies in the market. For Ahme, rather, it was a smell sweeter than any perfume, for it showed them the path to glory and riches.

It spread far beyond their shop. It could be smelled everywhere in the vicinity; anyone who came even within a few hundred metres of its source was overwhelmed by the nauseating stench of decay, and they would check their clothes and shoes in case they had stepped in something and hadn't noticed. Closer to the onion stockpile, the stench became stronger and stronger, and it made people think that they had no doubt happened upon a cistern full of sewage, or a dumping ground for carcasses that had been improperly slaughtered.

As the situation became more and more unbearable, the district administrator began to receive complaints. He summoned the "shitty Sufis", as he called them, to attend him immediately. When his men dragged Sufi Alo before him, the administrator shouted at him that he had screwed up badly, ordering him to dispose of all the onions in his possession; for, if he did not do so, the stench would consume the entire town, and perhaps attract some kind of infectious disease. Something that stank more horribly than manure could bring cholera upon them, or some other terrible calamity.

Afterwards Alo was left in the corridor outside the administrator's office. He sat down, waiting to be ordered to leave; but before he could even start thinking about what he would do about his situation, an errand boy came running down the corridor, shouting at the top of his lungs:

"It's on fire! The market's on fire!"

Alo saw indecision in the eyes of the administrator's men, and he decided to run, to see with his own eyes the disaster that would ruin him and drive him mad. He saw his shop burning in front of him and tried in vain to dive into the flames. But the onions were already gone.

He did not know who was responsible, but he knew what he had to do.

He returned home, hurt and dejected, humiliated by his dream that would now never come to pass, and that had turned into a wretched nightmare. His stockpile of onions had been ruined in front of his very eyes. He had neglected to guard the goods in which he had invested years and years of what he and his brother had earned, denying his family, confident that he would be able to provide all they needed and more after he had finished the deal of his life. And now here he was, his life's work obliterated. His dreams had turned to ash.

How would he bring the news to Ahme? And how would his brother respond, given the many warnings he had made about the consequences of unbridled greed for money in our short earthly lives? How would he justify it to his mother, who had removed herself completely from their sons' business, after she had satisfied herself that they were handling it well enough? Could he blame her for withdrawing her sage counsel, when he had closed his ears to all that anyone had said to him?

When he returned home, his family were all waiting outside. He looked exhausted and miserable, his cap in his arms, kneading it between his fingers as if he could take revenge on it for his troubles, or erase everyone from existence by ruining it. And of course, the first of these would be the district administrator, the idiot who had ruined his life and ordered him to dispose of his onions before morning.

"Ahmad. Please, come with me. I beg you, don't ask me about anything. Just give me a hand with this. I'll tell you everything on the way."

Alo led his brother to the scene of the blaze that had destroyed all of their hopes and dreams. Ahme remained silent, his features betraying little beyond his deep sense of failure and disappointment.

They could not find anyone who was willing to help them clean up the shop as the district administrator had ordered. Each took a sack of onions on his shoulder and carried it down to the river to throw it away. Ahme began to feel sorry for his brother - and for himself - and he chided him as they walked:

"Did I not tell you to say, if God wills it? But you made fun of God."

"The oppressor who flouts God, God will use for His revenge, then avenge Himself upon him. God will punish the oppressor for his wrongdoings to us."

"You were the one who did wrong! For yourself, and for us!"

"Now is not the time to twist words around."

"But what was it that destroyed us?! Was it because I'm a coward, as you said to me? Or was it your greed that you've been hiding from yourself, as I told you!"

"And how do you know what I was going to do? Was I not planning for the both of us? Oh, God forgive you. You don't know anything! But you still want you say that you warned me, and you explained, and and and -"

"God made the world in six days, and you want to make your world in one!"

"Ahme! Are you on my side or not?"

"I'm not on the side of greed. I told you many times that senseless greed will be the end of us. But you -"

"You may have said that. But on the inside, you agreed with me. You only had doubts about whether the deal would really go ahead. If it's true what you say, then why didn't you convince me you were right? Why didn't you sell the onions when you were in charge of the shop? Why were you running around with me so that we could get more and more? Well? Tell me!"

"Again! It's your mess that you're trying to stick to me. I told you so many times. I told you exactly how it was. But you played blind and deaf."

"Such wise words coming out of your mouth now. Where was your genius when we were nearly bankrupt?!"

They shouted at each other, exchanging the blame, while they carried out the ruined, half-burnt sacks of onions. The delivery boys refused to help them, and the administrator's men told them they needed to carry them far away from the market, away from the river and out beyond the edge of town, so as not to make the situation even worse.

All the hatred and resentment that had accumulated between them began to seep out. They might have thought they had forgotten it, but, in their hearts, they were still nursing all the grievances they'd accumulated during the time they were in business together. Secretly, the resentment grew, without them being fully aware of it. All the little things they had previously ignored now came out into the open, a subject for endless squabbles. These in turn became big problems, problems that could never be solved. This began to spoil their brotherly relationship, and when one of them felt rejected by the other, he responded in kind.

They began to keep score for every slight, big or small, that they could remember. They had little goodwill or forgiveness left for each other. They replaced it with blame and recrimination for every single thing that was said, and everything that had happened.

As far as the town was concerned, they were laughingstocks. They were now known by any number of unpleasant nicknames: the Bifazo Sufis, or the Onion Lords, the Shitty Sufis . . . or just Smelly Onions to some.

They had spent an entire day moving the spoiled onions out to a deserted place on the outskirts of town. When they could finally start to burn them, Sufi Alo positioned himself next to the flames, and pissed on them standing up, unlike his normal position. He said nothing as he stood motionless, his unblinking gaze fixed on the flames that were devouring his past and his present and his future.

They returned home in silence, one behind the other. The exhaustion on their faces was clear. Their deep sorrow and pain, though unexpressed, had begun to creep into their hearts. Tears gathered in the corners of their eyes, but refused to fall, as if the soil beneath them should be refused the rain for which it longed after seasons of drought and failed harvests. The shame and dishonour that they had suffered had opened a gulf between them that might never again be bridged.

Now, their lives would begin to diverge. Their working partnership, once so strong, had all but disintegrated; it had poisoned their brotherly feelings. What had once bound them together now divided them, even as they had nobody else to depend on but each other.

Perhaps they should have looked for different paths from the beginning. Close paths, perhaps; but not the same one, for that would eventually become too narrow for them both. In any business, it was preferable to avoid partnership; for if it were otherwise, would not God Himself have found a partner? Had they realised this, they would each have had to work on their own, and not together. They might have been able to preserve their love and brotherly bond through help and advice, while never sharing their money.

But how could they have? They were but two orphans, offspring of a mountain tragedy that had forced their mother to take them and leave her home.

We are all victims, Alo thought, with a bitterness in his mouth, and a sorrow on his face that he could no longer hide. Victims, disguised as executioners. Sheep in wolves' clothing.

Word of the burning of the onions spread through town, and to the villages beyond. Those who liked to exaggerate named that year "the Year of the Burning of the Onions". And so it came to rank with all the other famous Years of popular imagination - like the Year of the Commotion, or the Year of the Burning of the Cinema, or, before them, the Year of Red Snow. Or heavy snow, as some older people still insisted on calling it.

Chapter 9

After that terrible day, Ahme stayed at home and never left the house - apart from once, when he wasn't out for long, and nobody knew where he had been. His sad predicament filled his mother's mind, especially because he would refuse all her attempts to approach and comfort him. He would only repeat: "Thanks and praise be to God, a thousand times, and I'm not angry about what happened."

He was, in fact, sincere in what he was saying. But as time went on, he became more and more irritable. He retreated into himself and would no longer attend the congregational prayers at the mosque. He still wouldn't miss the Friday prayer, but he went and prayed in the back row, and then he left before everyone else. Most people never even saw him.

Still, after the prayer, one of the worshippers managed to catch up with Ahme, and told him: "Be ready tonight. After dinner."

Concise and to the point. Not a single word more than was needed.

"I'm ready," Ahme replied.

It was the night when they would cross the border into Turkey. The message came from a smuggler who had agreed to help Ahme leave the town, after Ahme had begged him. He wanted to cross the border and get to Serxete, and he didn't care if it was heaven or hellfire waiting for him on the other side. When the smuggler asked where exactly he was headed, he said he didn't know; he just wanted to get away, and quickly. He would decide later.

The smuggler promised to get back to him in a matter of days, and it was in fact less than a week before he was told to get ready. But Ahme still had had plenty of time to think about where he would go.

After dinner, Ahme rose to leave. He ignored his brother and his mother, he passed his brother's wife, who was reading the Holy Quran and oblivious to everything, and he bent down to kiss the sleeping Hawar on his cheeks and then his forehead.

He did not turn around or say anything at all. His decision was final, and he would not change his mind, whatever happened. No amount of pleading would sway him. It was his fate to leave. Nothing bound him to this place any longer. He didn't mind leaving his mother, or his brother. It only broke his heart to be leaving Hawar. How would he stand being apart from him? This boy was his beating heart, his only hope in the world, the light that brightened his darkest days. Hawar's laughter cured all of Ahme's ills; his joy and playfulness chased away all the disasters that life had inflicted on him.

But Ahme reined in his emotions. He wished for Hawar to relish his childhood - unlike his own, which he had never managed to enjoy. He wished for him to grow up by the favour and grace of God, and that God would reward him with a prosperous life.

His companions that night welcomed him with jokes and mockery.

"Ah, Sufi Ahme!" their leader said. "So you decided to leave the Sufis and join the smugglers? Perhaps you've discovered that we avoid confrontation and always postpone everything to the hereafter?"

"I think," another said, "that he realised that our life is full of excitement and adventure . . . and much nicer and happier than the monotonous existence of a Sufi!"

"You've escaped from yourself!" a third said, laughing. "Very well done."

Ahme only greeted them politely. He didn't reply to their comments; he knew they were good men at heart and didn't mean to hurt or insult him.

He was the last one they were waiting for. They'd gathered at a hill that wasn't more than a few kilometres outside of town; they were all well used to the journey - apart, of course, from Ahme, tonight's "special guest". It would be his first crossing - or at least, the first one in many years, ever since he had crossed with his mother, his brother, and their black goat, when they first came to Amouda, where their mother thought she could seek refuge with her sons. They had crossed the border looking for a place his mother had chosen, fleeing from a place she never named, and which she had refused to talk about since.

When he now remembered his last crossing, in the opposite direction, it was like a distant dream from a completely different life, or a half-forgotten tale. They hadn't needed to do anything other than tell the border guard that they were merely going back home, as they had spent the day at their uncle's house. When the guard pointed out that his colleague hadn't informed him of this, their mother quickly improvised; she was determined to cross. "Surely," she said, "he just forgot to tell you."

And while Ahme might have been their guest, he received no special treatment because of it. To them, honouring a guest meant accepting him completely into the group - even if only for one trip. So he was given a bag to carry on his back. He did so gladly, even though he had no idea what was in it; he didn't ask, as he didn't want to draw attention to himself. He sought refuge in silence, as well as his total observance of the orders and instructions that he received. These included orders that were customary in such situations, such as hiding when one of them sensed the approach of a light or a person, hurrying along when told to do so, and other orders that were part of the ancient arts of care and caution.

He fought against the exhaustion that began to creep over him. The load they had him carry on his back was heavy, but he had an even bigger, heavier burden to worry about, and that consumed and exhausted him even more.

They arrived at the agreed-upon location, between the hill of Hamdoune and that strange village of strange people who never seemed to be able to fully integrate with the locals. There was a small dry stream there that filled up with water after the winter rains. After they had crossed it, Ahme noticed that the smugglers had covered it up with thorn bushes, to hide the gaps in the barbed wire that had been put down on the Turkish side, and to provide some natural-looking cover for their frequent crossings.

They waited for a sign from their ringleader, who had gone out towards the border. It did not take them long before, shortly after midnight, the crossing was completed, with skill and professionalism. They filed after the ringleader in a clear, zig-zagging line, and Ahme was the only one who kept looking around and hesitating, to the extent that the man behind him had to warn him to look straight ahead and focus on keeping to the line.

He was surprised by what he saw. He had expected a somewhat different experience from the last time he had crossed, and which he wanted to forget. He had heard recently about tensions on the border, and shots fired between the smugglers and the army, with casualties on both sides. He did not hide from himself or his brother Alo his disgust at the unwritten law of the smugglers, which stipulated that you should not wait for anyone who stops, and he asked God's forgiveness whenever he heard that a smuggler had killed one of his comrades after a heated discussion about somebody falling behind.

But this time, it seemed as if by chance one of the border guards had, at that very moment, left his post to relieve himself. When he was done, he picked up a stone from the ground, as if looking for something to wipe his arse with; but while doing so, he turned his back to them and stayed in that position, leaving them in the clear. At the same time, the guard at the other end stayed far out near the line of the horizon, wandering around like he was searching for something he had lost. He kept at it until they had crossed over the two hundred metres by one. Then he went back to his post, as if nothing at all had happened.

Ahme likewise didn't notice anyone from the group reaching for the guns they had hanging from their chest - each with two full magazines and a spare - except for their leader at the head of the column, who led them on and away from the border, behind a small hill. There Ahme's wonder only grew when he saw another group of men approaching. They exchanged a set of signals with the ringleader, then came closer and began to exchange greetings and kisses.

One of the men from the other group must have noticed a new face, and he made a remark about Ahme's presence.

"Sufi Ahme is an honourable man," the ringleader said to reassure him. "A special guest, no more. You shouldn't doubt him."

"If the leader trusts him and can vouch for him," another man from the other group said, "then surely there's no cause for worry."

They handed over their goods. They should hurry back, they said, before they ran out of time. The ringleader urged the other group to take good care of Sufi Ahme, adding that it was very important to him personally that they respect Ahme's wishes and deliver him to wherever he wanted to go.

Ahme hardly had time to thank them, for they picked up their bags and made to leave, wishing luck to their comrades, and to Ahme as well.

"So now you know," the ringleader murmured to Ahme, "what the smuggler's life is like! But try not to get too addicted to these adventures, for they are not what they seem. Go back to your life and stay happy and content with your mosque and your prayers. It's much better that way. In this job, we only have two choices in the end: the grave or the prison cell. Stay well."

The ringleader wanted to tell him about other difficulties, like the fact that, if he did not end up with one of the two ends he mentioned, then he would surely end up in hunger and poverty. For smuggling is not a profession; it is, rather, a crime, to which one is pushed by other, more terrible crimes, which are themselves the end results of this crime - that is, hunger and poverty. Or perhaps he would tell him about how easy it was to get addicted to smuggling, kindled by an endless smouldering blaze. But he could not say any of this out loud, because they didn't have time.

As they left, Ahme felt a pain in his heart and a renewed bitterness in his mouth. He felt like the smell of his home was fading away, the sound of Hawar's laughter retreating with it. Still, when a man from the new group asked where he was headed, he answered immediately:

"To Qarashike."

"Which one, though?" the man asked.

Ahme hesitated. He had no idea what to say; he knew of only one village called Qarashike. But the question meant there must have been another Qarashike.

"It's close," he said, tentatively, "to Dare."

"They're both close to Dare, my dear Sufi," the smuggler said, with a grin on his face. "You mean the upper Qarashike? They call it Aydin now, in Turkish. The sons of bitches changed the names of all our villages, so none of us can remember how to call them! Don't worry about it. I get it."

They changed all the names on our side, too, Ahme thought of saying; and most people didn't know what their village was called, either. But, as usual, he kept his retort to himself. It might have sounded as if he were trying to be clever, speaking when he shouldn't. He wanted to steer clear of any possible awkwardness, and certainly he didn't want to make himself the centre of attention.

They walked until they reached a fair distance from the border, crossing the highway that linked Nusaybin to Kiziltepe and the threshing grounds of the village of Kundik.

"We have to go our separate ways now," the smuggler said. He pointed Ahme to a light on the hillside before them. "Walk toward that light, exactly toward it, in a straight line, and you'll get to where you want. Qarashike is that way - it's the first village you'll reach."

Sufi Ahme thanked them for their help, the way he had wanted to thank the ringleader, although that had not been possible due to the speed with which they had parted ways. He wished them all the best of luck and set out on the path that had been pointed out to him.

"No need for us to remind you," said the smuggler, as they set out north, "but do trust the ringleader . . . as we trust him, and his protection."

Chapter 10

He thought it was a monster of some sort. He froze in place, too scared to approach. As he took a closer look at it, he realised it was a stray cow that looked as though it had gotten lost on its way home, or perhaps fallen behind the rest of the herd. He ran after it, and only with the utmost effort managed to grasp the rope around its neck. He tried to calm it with murmured words whose origin or significance he didn't know; they were only noises, calming sounds that he slowed down and then sped up, and he soon realised he wasn't sure what he was trying to achieve with them.

He sat down for a while and asked God's forgiveness. He decided to take the cow to the village, which he realised had to be close now. He could feel it in the sloping of the ground, and even more so in the marshy ground to the north, which looked just as it always had, with a huge heap of rubbish rising out of it.

Not much had changed about the village, apart from a few houses that had sprung up at the far end. He would realise later that these belonged to men who had moved away from their families after getting married and built their own houses nearby. This did not require particular skill to deduce; few outsiders came to the village, and there was nobody at all from the city apart from the teacher - during the school year - and the preacher, who gave the sermon on Fridays. And, of course, the travelling merchants - and the villagers knew precisely when they would arrive.

He entered the village just as the dawn call to prayer began. He headed immediately toward the mosque, distinguished from the other buildings by the green crescent lit up on its roof. The mosque was small inside, no bigger than a large room, and its courtyard, enclosed by a low wall, was about as big as its interior. He tied the cow to a dried-out tree trunk close to the mosque.

"I seek refuge with God from the accursed Satan," he muttered, "in the name of God, the Merciful, the Compassionate."

Although he was exhausted, his heart drew him inside the mosque, and he entered the courtyard in a state of perfect calm. He filled a jug with water from the barrel, then headed to the basin in the corner to perform his ablutions; this relaxed him even further.

When the mullah heard the noises outside, he hurried out of the mosque, for he knew that none of the villagers would come for morning prayer. He was shocked to see the cow tied up right outside, but his shock was even greater when he saw a man sitting in the yard, his legs stretched out after his ablutions. He greeted him, then invited him in.

He welcomed the visitor, quickly scrutinised his features, then commenced the prayer. The mullah led, and the man prayed after him. They were the only ones in the mosque.

They finished the prayer, and each muttered his own supplications to God. After a few moments of silence, the mullah said: "Where have you come from? And where are you going?"

At first, Ahme didn't answer. He could see how surprised the mullah was upon seeing the cow, which he'd realised was in fact very similar to the cow that he owned. So Ahme began by telling him how he had come across the poor lost beast, and what he had done with it- having no idea that it was, in fact, the mullah's own cow, and his only cow, which he depended on for his livelihood.

"I am Sufi Ahme," he told the mullah, finally, "from Binxate. I come from Amouda, and I came here because I'm headed here, to your village." He didn't know what else to say.

"Welcome, then, my son," the mullah replied. "I thank you for your honesty, and for the trouble you have gone to in order to bring the cow back. You are my guest for as long as you're in the village."

The mullah had no more questions for him, but Ahme nevertheless went on. "I am the son of Khatoune of Jayaye," he explained, "and we settled in Amouda more than twenty-five years ago. Before that, we travelled around. We were in all the villages of Jayaye Omriyan. We stayed for a while in every village we passed through . . . and your village was one of them. Here, we stayed at the house of Najibo Qarashiki. He was a good man. He is a relative of Sufi Farho, from Amouda, who is the father-in-law of my older brother Sufi Alo -"

"Najibo Qarashiki, may God rest his soul! He truly was a good man. Now, I remember your mother. She was a very special woman. Back then, she never told anyone about her secret. . . and she didn't tell you about it either, my son?"

The mullah spoke as if he were judging history for its misdeeds, recalling events from the distant past that he hadn't thought he would tell anyone about every again - all the more so because people nowadays were preoccupied with work, desperate to secure their families' livelihood. The goodness that had enriched those days was fading away, bit by bit. Young people had begun to abandon religion, and to amuse themselves with frivolous things.

The mullah did not even notice that Sufi Ahme had not answered his question; he went on, in a trembling voice that rose and fell quickly from the bottom of his chest, showing his more than eighty years of age: "I have served this little mosque, my son, for many years, carrying out my duties towards my Lord. I settled here with my wife and my daughter after we'd been made homeless when the army burnt down my village in retaliation for the revolt. They punished those villages that wouldn't submit to their humiliation, but they burnt down other villages as well, those that supported them. Oh, my son. You see, the villagers here gave us shelter for a few months, but then the pains came over my wife, and I lost her, along with my unborn son. And from that day, I have dedicated myself to the service of God."

It was as if the mullah had been waiting for someone to come along to whom he could talk about the years that he had spent in silence, and he was now reciting his last will and testament. Or perhaps he was taking revenge for the past that had silenced him, and the injustice that he hoped to be compensated for in the afterlife. But before he finished his story of silence and seclusion, he realised that he had been speaking for long enough. He had been blessed by a kind companion, after being abandoned for so long, much like the mosque to which he had pledged himself; he would have been forgotten were it not for the misfortunes that befell people every now and then. He remembered others who hurried to him for comfort, and words that gave them hope, and consolation for their troubles through vague promises that did nothing but calm the surface of their distress. But he liked Sufi Ahme, and his speech gained an affectionate tone, for he appreciated his honesty in bringing back the cow that he could just as easily have run away with.

"But, my son," the mullah said, "why do I bother you now with these troubles? Surely you are yourself fleeing some great tragedy? If you would like to tell me about it, know that I am your uncle and your brother, in your faith, and in the order and the Path. And I can help you. The children of Najibo Qarashiki, God rest his soul, have left this place. You are my guest now. Let's go home, and rest a little, and we'll have time to talk about everything later."

He didn't give Ahme much choice in the matter. "Come!" he ordered, as he set out ahead of him. "Sayre, my daughter, will have finished baking the bread."

Ahme had not smoked in a while, and so by now his stomach was growling with hunger. He was trying his best not to collapse and did not hesitate to follow the mullah; it would have been a grave sin to question his orders, as Ahme was just passing through and was obliged to honour his host.

The mullah stopped a few steps away from his house, clearing his throat. Then he called out for his daughter and told her to hurry with breakfast, for they had a very dear guest come to visit them.

That is how they had always used to do it: receiving guests gladly and generously, feeding them the same food that they ate. But years of estrangement, or "dependence" as he might describe it, had made the mullah an outsider toward whom the villagers acted charitably, while nobody ever visited his home. They would invite him into their homes, or visit him at the mosque - where he was usually to be found in any case - even though they had given him the cattle to secure a livelihood for him and his daughter.

Ahme followed him with some hesitation. But the smell of freshly baked bread was overwhelming, and he felt as if his bones had shrivelled from hunger. When he lowered his gaze to greet Sayre, he nearly collapsed from dizziness. "Peace be upon you, my daughter," he said, but he heard nothing in response from her, for she only muttered her greeting in a very quiet voice before hurrying into the kitchen to prepare breakfast.

All the villagers would hear about the arrival of a guest who intended to settle in their village. The young heard from the old, and the old heard from each other. It became their biggest preoccupation. The story of Grandma Khatoune became known once more, after it had been all but forgotten. Information about her and her sons proliferated and spread until it became known to all, rebutted by the efforts of a few who speculated: "They are, without a doubt, from this village, or from that tribe." Because they looked like those people, or had crossed paths with them, or lived nearby.

The arguments they developed were not, however, particularly convincing. They were not precise, or based in fact, but rather depended on feelings or fleeting impressions, or the similarity of someone's character to that of someone else in this or that tribe.

Ahme stayed as the mullah's guest for four days. The mullah did not allow anybody else to host him, for Ahme was his brother in the order and the Path, and he carried with him the virtuous spirit of his sheikh. During those four days, they spoke about many things, but most of all about the past because, for them, everything was oriented toward the past, and the only future was that of the afterlife.

On the dawn of the fifth day, the mullah felt too weak to go to the mosque for the call to prayer. He was much distressed and worried by this, for he had never before neglected his duty in the service of God, not even for a single day. But Sufi Ahme put an arm around his shoulders and said:

"God bless you, uncle, but you are truly among the best of God's servants, and those most close to him. God willing, your place will be in heaven!"

He then helped Sayre lay the mullah down on his bed and turned him to face Mecca, just as he requested. Then the mullah made another request to Ahme: "I would like you to call in my place."

"I will call in your place this dawn," Ahme said, to comfort him. "But, God willing, you will be calling at noon."

Ahme called that dawn, and he called on all other dawns that followed. For when he hurried back from his prayer that morning, he found the mullah lying still and unmoving on his bed, muttering his prayer. Ahme could not find his daughter anywhere in the house, but after a while, he heard voices outside - the voice of the village mayor, and his son - both of whom the mullah had sent for, so they could hear his final testament. Ahme felt as though he had been struck by lightning; he could not believe what he was hearing, and he had to go outside, not knowing what to do.

"I swear to you, mayor, that I leave everything that I have to my brother, Sufi Ahme. And I give him leave to marry my daughter Sayre. I trust them in your care, and that's all I ask of you, mayor. Promise to do what I ask. Do you promise me?"

"I promise you, mullah," the mayor assured him. "I promise you. But, by God's will, you will get out of bed again, and you won't need to entrust anyone with what you intend to do."

"I close my eyes now, and I know the mosque is in good care, and my daughter. Thank you so much, mayor."

The mullah said that, then twice bore witness to God, and closed his eyes in peace.

Silence fell over the house, pierced by a loud cry from Sayre, followed by her muffled sobbing, and a torrent of tears that nobody there knew how to stop.

The mullah's will was carried out, and Ahme married Sayre. He did not know exactly how old she was, and he didn't try to guess. But she was certainly older than him, according to what people said in the village. He lived in the mullah's house and took over the mosque. Between the calls to prayer, he herded the animals that the mullah had owned, and that had passed to him as well. These now provided for his and his wife's livelihood, in addition to the occasional donation from the villagers and the mayor - which was not considered formally as zakat, but mostly came from feelings of brotherhood and obligation.

Mullah Ahme Benxati, as he came to be known, slowly grew used to his new life. He swore that he would never forget his friend the old mullah and pledged himself and his wife to fulfil all the man's wishes. This started with the mosque, which he renovated and improved into the shape it has today. The villagers helped him in this endeavour, after he told them that whoever helps in building a house of God, God will build palaces for them in Heaven. For the old mosque was, in truth, dilapidated. And he took care of the chickens which had been so dear to the old mullah, who was always accompanied by animals, in some way.

Ahme tried to rein in the memories that now and then threatened to overwhelm him. The worst were memories of little Hawar, and the times he had played with him. Tears would suddenly flow from his eyes as he was tending to his flock down in the plain, and he would ask forgiveness for Hawar, and for his ignorance. For he remembered well how his hopes had been shattered when the simple questions that confused him had been answered, and when the doubts that had crept into his heart when these were being discussed were dispelled, by the warnings and reprimands of a certain Faqqih Abd al-Wahhab.

Chapter 11

Ahme slept in the living room for forty days after the death of the mullah, while his wife slept in the bedroom. The forty-first night was a Thursday. Ahme stayed behind to busy himself in the mosque, then went to the mayor's house, and stayed there with the others until the end of the evening's gathering. Then he went home. When he entered the living room, his mattress wasn't there. He panicked at first, thinking that something had happened to his wife, for she had never before forgotten to make or clean his bed. He knocked on the wooden door which separated the bedroom from the front living room and went in.

He was completely overcome with embarrassment, the deep kind of shyness that becomes a menace to whomever feels it, even though he knew that shyness was reprehensible in a man, while it was desirable in a woman. Folk wisdom confirms this, through the proverb: "A shy woman is worth a whole village; a shy man is just a coward." Even so, Ahme clung on to his timidity, neither making an approach nor indicating that he would like to with his actions or movements.

After his wife had given up all hope of him doing anything, she took the initiative herself. She took her neighbour's advice that they sleep in a single bed - though more details had not been provided. Still, she gave it a go, even though she did not really know what she should be doing.

Ahme was, likewise, ignorant in these matters. He'd never once been alone with a woman and had always suppressed his wants and desires, seeking God's protection from the temptations of the flesh and neglecting much that went on in his body. So he was surprised when he saw that his wife had prepared them a meal that was lavish by their standards: chicken on a plate of bulghur, with yoghurt and vegetables. He was even more surprised to see what his wife looked like. She had changed out of her faded black clothes and put on a red dress with coloured embroidery, patched with a square of white cloth on its lower left side. She looked like a lost sorceress. Her uncovered neck stretched out, her head held high, rather than kept it down as it usually was. Ahme had noticed the patch on the dress not because he was looking for it, but merely because he was so quick to focus his gaze on the ground, too embarrassed to look in the eyes of his wife, who had undergone this sudden transformation. He realised she was gesturing for him, cautiously, to start eating his dinner, so it wouldn't get cold a third time. She'd had to warm it up twice already because he had been so late.

Ahme understood her urgency and began to move. He washed his face and his hands, praying to the Prophet a number of times and invoking God's name. He then approached the table, hoping his wife would join him. He felt a strange sense of elation spread through his body and tried to suppress it as he normally would, but his hunger was stronger than his will. He ate like he'd never eaten before. The desire that had slept deep in the confines of his soul and body had finally been awakened. He imagined his wife was the chicken that he was eating: he would part the flesh of her thighs; he would sink his teeth into her white breast and break it into pieces before finishing it off. He had the yoghurt to round off his meal; it only invigorated him further.

The tea, after all this food, was the greatest joy of all. He relished drinking it together with his wife and talking about the animals, especially the health of the new kid goat, and bits of gossip about the villagers. Though soon enough he no longer really heard what she was saying, just as she didn't want to explain the things he was asking about;. They were both completely preoccupied with what would happen that night.

"So where will you sleep, Ahmad?" she asked, and took a sip of tea.

She was very interested in his answer and very concerned about what he would say, without wanting to give any of that away. She had already decided, of course, that he would sleep next to her, but it seemed that she could never quite free herself from the idea that, as a woman, she was to be wanted and desired, and not to be the one who initiated things. Women learned this was in their very nature; they were not necessarily taught it in school, nor did they hear the information from someone in particular, or learn it from a book, or were otherwise formally educated in it. They were, rather, taught by the reality of their lives, in which nobody was given a choice. Many village women, and especially older ones, were not ashamed to speak about sex among themselves, or even in gatherings where men were present. They would disclose the most private details, cursing and swearing throughout. This made the younger women blush and avert their eyes - though, on the inside, they would be sniggering along with everyone else. They only pretended to be embarrassed, while really they wanted the talk to go on, as they loved to hear about this outwardly forbidden subject.

She went briefly into the kitchen attached to the living room. This room also served as their shower room, by way of a simple adjustment: setting aside an area of about a metre's-width from the door and calling it a "washroom." This was the case in many of the clay houses whose inhabitants called the corner meant for washing and bathing the "sarshouk": the water could run out easily through a small hole at the bottom of the corner, after the floor had been sloped and paved with cement so that the water didn't accumulate. It was only a slightly more civilised arrangement than the one Ahme had enjoyed in their house in Amouda.

"Aren't you going to change?" she asked when she came back. She would not look into his eyes. "I brought out my father's clean clothes. They're in the front room."

So she was inviting him into her bed. Why wait, then, when she was his wife? There was no sin in it! He got up, with some enthusiasm, and went to wash himself. His heart was pounding when he stepped into the living room to change. She had put out a small bottle of cologne next to the clothes, so he could dab it on. The scent was one he had worn before; this excited him further. He hastened to praise his Lord and thank Him for the blessings that He had bestowed upon him. He didn't mind that the old mullah's clothes were a little tight on him. They made him look a little younger, in fact; or perhaps they only showed his true age, rather than the pretend venerability given him by the clothes he usually wore, which made him look at least a decade older.

When he returned to the bedroom, his wife had already put out the big lamp and left the smaller one burning with a soft light. She had also laid out a rug for him next to the bed. She herself had, meanwhile, snuck into the bed, and was now lying stretched out on her back, her gaze directed at the ceiling. Strange, conflicting feelings welled up in her soul; she felt like she never had before, and it seemed to be a mix of all possible emotions, which confused her even more.

Her husband, meanwhile, had drifted away. He professed God's name and kept repeating the Throne Verse. After the pleasant feelings that had befallen him when he entered the room, he now felt he was on the threshold of entering Heaven itself. Was he really seeing this? The bedroom, in its soft light, looked like it had turned into a city that contained everything a man could ever desire. The light fell on the rug, and he quickly knelt to prostrate twice according to the pious custom of one's marriage night. His mind wandered, he was distracted, and he did not perform the movements correctly. He had to do them again. He also nearly forgot to say his supplications of forgiveness and hope, and to humble himself over his wishes and desires, as most of this concerned the afterlife and was only linked by invisible threads to his earthly existence.

After he was satisfied that he had performed his duty toward his Lord, he turned to perform his duty towards his wife. He approached the bed, doing his utmost to hide his confusion and the fumbling movements of his body. The trembling in his joints and the shiver in his jaw nearly betrayed him, and he tried to compose himself by recalling certain sayings of the Prophet that he had heard in the marketplace. Before, he had condemned saying them out loud, though he would always listen for them, because he thought that they would help him on his wedding night. But he could not remember a single word or phrase from them. His mind had betrayed him, even before his body could.

Silence hung between them. He cursed himself and his negligence; it was as if his tongue had been tied, and there was no other way for him to speak. He realised his wife had removed her headscarf, which she would otherwise wear day and night; Ahme found her hair extremely alluring, and the sight of it excited him so much it embarrassed him, even on this blessed Thursday night. He praised God yet again.

He gathered all his strength, as if he were trying to stare down an enemy by focusing his gaze on them. He focused all his thoughts on the movements that he was supposed to make; like touching his foot to hers, perhaps. Slowly, very slowly, their bodies began to draw closer; silence reigned over them, as did the concealing veil of darkness. He thanked her silently for having turned down the light, so it wouldn't reveal his nakedness. He was afraid of seeing his body in its current state, and even more so of seeing hers—this body that he was obliged to do something with.

And was she not his labour: the soil he would plough, his property, his fortune? So why was he afraid?

Ahme felt a dizziness come over him. He didn't know how he ended up turning over to embrace his wife, and started kissing her all over her face, drawing in her tongue and lips. Doing this gave him a thrill, and he closed his eyes. He didn't need to look for her lips, and it seemed as if, of their own accord, their mouths had closed together, and their wet tongues wrapped around each other. He ignored the careful and gentle caresses, the warm, quiet whispers. The thin light was fading. He felt himself engrossed in a struggle with his body that he had detested, and his spirit that he had repressed. He was rebellious, disoriented, bursting with madness, and he didn't notice that his penis had stayed flabby, and had not risen or tightened up like the rest of his body. He would nearly have lost consciousness in his maddened daze, if his wife hadn't given him a soft push that brought him back to his senses. Even through her closed eyes, she saw in him the likeness of her father: his clothes that she still secretly feared, and his piercing scent that always betrayed his presence. She cursed herself a thousand times for letting herself imagine her father was the one kissing or touching her; her conscience pained her for letting such terrible thoughts creep into her mind. But she could not control her imagination, or the disgusting images that it brought into being and revealed to her.

He wasn't fully aware of the awkwardness his penis might cause. She asked him, a little reprovingly, to take his clothes off, and while he was doing this, she shuffled under the duvet to take off her outer robe, while she kept on her short-sleeved undergown. Meanwhile, Ahme pulled off his trousers and touched his penis imploringly. He realised that he had, in the throes of passion, forgotten to prepare himself properly, and had not shaved his pubic hair which now hung loose and threatened to completely cover the penis while it was in its flaccid state.

Their haphazard touches and caresses did not do much to bring them closer; for they could not join two bodies that had been, ever since their birth, slaves to repression and silence, and had indeed been passed down through generations - from grandfather to father, from mother to daughter.

Ahme only came to when he felt sunlight falling on his face. He forced his eyes open, and then jumped out of bed as if he had been stung by a bee. He poked his head out of the front door and saw that the village was already bustling with activity. This was the only time when he had not called for prayer at dawn; sleep had overpowered him, even as, through the night, he had kept fighting it, struck by waves of cold sweat while his heart pounded and his muscles cramped.

"You call every dawn," Sayre said, "but nobody prays in the mosque. They all get up, but they can't be bothered to come to their mosque or to do their prayers!"

She tried to alleviate his annoyance at himself for his waywardness. She moved herself closer to him, laid a hand on his head, and stroked his back. She was still wearing her nightdress; there were no more secrets between their bodies, after they had endured their first night together, which had gone a long way toward bridging the distance between them.

Ahme didn't overly regret his failures of the previous night - and certainly not to the extent that he would miss the dawn prayer. He tortured himself over this, and thus he probably underestimated the tragic extent of his failure, on a night that a man should see as the night of his life, consuming himself in his yearning and desire for it. But despite all this, he felt a calm spread through him as Sayre spoke to him; not so much from her words as from her rubbing of his head and her touch on his back. She had broken all the barriers between them, surrendering to him all her yearning, love, desire, and sympathy.

The nights that followed made it possible for their bodies to finally draw closer, joining and coming together in the way they desired. But the passing years did not grant them a child that would fill up their world. So they grew estranged from each other once again, miserable in the monotony of their daily lives.

Chapter 12

"It is not the skullcap that makes a true Sufi, or the prayer beads, or the beard. Sufi Alo, the most important thing is your heart. Keep it pure, keep it pious, and ask God for forgiveness. Don't you know that hoarders are to be cursed? And yet you are determined to lead us into damnation . . . or, indeed, to bring it to us!"

Sufi Alo would never forget his brother's words. They rang in his ears and in his heart. He would repeat them to himself, sometimes in his brother's voice, exactly as he had said them, or sometimes in a different, more agitated tone. Each time he repeated them, their weight on him grew heavier, penetrating into the deepest recesses of his soul. He began to talk to himself aloud: he would extol the wisdom of his brother's words and the overflowing kindness of his heart that had led him into foolishness and concealed what was undoubtedly Satan's attemps to mislead him, and which would bring dire consequences. His admiration for his brother knew no bounds: things had been revealed to him - so Alo would say - and he was one of the saints and mystics who truly were close to God, hidden among the masses of the poor and unwashed. And though he was illiterate, Alo said, he possessed knowledge imparted to him by God Himself - and these were words that the Sufis usually reserved for their most respected sheikhs.

Ahme's absence had turned him into a wise man and a saint. He was ascribed qualities that he could never have dreamed of, those of a man who could see to the very essence of things and reveal their hidden dimensions to others. In his brother's eyes, he could only rise higher and higher.

The virtue of distance is that it purifies and softens the heart. It ensures that things once hidden from view are revealed, hatreds put aside. It allows one to link things together in ways that would normally look strange, but which are completely convincing to whomever discovers them. This is how distance works. But when the true reason behind the admiration is revealed, the status of the absent person returns to what it once was. This might, in their own view as well as that of their admirers, cast them down far lower than they thought they deserved. But in thinking this way, they would be trying to escape from a reality that ultimately could not be hidden. However tangled their thought processes might be, they could never prevent their thoughts from eventually clearing, and creating a truer, more faithful image of the absent person. And that is what would persist in memory, and in the real world.

Alo's days at home made him feel as if he had been locked for years in solitary confinement. He felt all the more imprisoned because he wasn't used to spending time at home. For much of his life, he'd preferred the bustle outside, and especially the market; now, he felt it urging him to overcome the catastrophe that had befallen him, in his foolish greed and ignorance. The home, moreover, had its needs, and it required someone to provide for it. Children don't understand the reasons behind want and poverty: and childhood should be a time of innocence, not worrying about one's financial situation. A child knows only that their needs must be met; they do not care how, and they wouldn't understand it.

Grandma Khatoune's kindness helped to calm her son's worries and give him strength. He was alone, now, after his brother's departure, and he shouldn't be keeping himself secluded at home like a woman. He was a father, and it would be the greatest possible humiliation if his child were to go hungry, or if the family wasn't able to meet its needs. A man should be able to take responsibility for his actions. There was no action without consequence, and he would have to pay the price for what he had done, however high it might be. His brother had left; his child was hungry; and his wife had finally lost her hearing completely, retreating into a world of silent ghosts. But his mother, even as her advancing years had weakened her, was still able to resist the trials and tribulations of earthly life. These trials had reached dizzying heights, but she was a daughter of the mountains, and she was never intimidated by them. Rather, she stood firm against the cruelty of life, satisfied that it was her fate to do so. Throughout her life, she had tried her utmost to change her destiny, and that of her sons, forever searching for a place that would grant them a decent life, one without resentments and machinations. But she had not found it, and her dreams would never come true. Or so she told herself in her darkest moments.

After the two disasters that he had suffered - the devastating loss of his business, and the heart-rending loss of his brother - Alo began to suffer from lack of sleep. He would stay up late and wake up early. People used to call him a "chicken," because he would go to sleep early, right after the night prayer. But now he stayed up until midnight, waking up before dawn.

He would stay at home and perform the prayers that he needed, and those that he had missed. And he never tired of beseeching God and repeating His name.

Having spent some time hiding himself away, one day Alo all of a sudden decided to pay a dawn visit to the bakery. He wanted to change his environment, to talk about his worries to the street as he walked along it, to enjoy some freshly baked bread and share it with his family. He wanted to break down the walls of sorrow that he had built around himself and to end the aversion to food that had afflicted him.

When he went to dress himself, he discovered that his wife had put his clothes into the washtub and left them to soak; she couldn't stand unpleasant smells, and she had planned to dry them in the morning. So Alo had to go and wake his mother. He told her that he would be the one to get the bread that morning, which she was very happy to hear. She found a pair of fertiliser bags, which still smelled strongly of urea, and stitched them up for him to wear as trousers. Alo told himself that the townspeople would surely still all be asleep. Still, he had to hurry, and to make good use of the time before the dawn call to prayer.

But when he got to the bakery, he saw that there were already a number of people waiting there, who were most certainly not asleep. He had no choice but to join the queue. The baker was quick to notice his peculiar outfit. When Sufi Alo tried to urge him to hand over the bread, he just told him to wait.

Alo had foolishly thought getting the bread would be an easy task. It turned out to be anything but. Soon a large crowd gathered in front of the bakery, young and old, women and men. He was extremely embarrassed. It would be a disaster to leave without the bread, but an even bigger one to have to stick around for much longer. The people began to whisper among themselves, and every newcomer asked the crowd why Sufi Bifazo was standing there half-naked like a plucked chicken. Alo, meanwhile, kept repeating to himself: my outfit is lawful in God's eyes; I can pray in it if I want to.

Nobody asked him for an explanation. They all averted their eyes, praised God's strength, and asked for His protection from whatever had struck this poor, miserable man.

Voices rose and fell:

"What happened to him?"

"Do people go mad like that when they lose all their money? He's not right, the poor man's gone crazy."

"You should fear God! Cover yourself, man, and hide yourself from your children."

"Two hits on the head must hurt quite a lot!"

While they criticised and abused him- directly or indirectly - Alo cursed his luck, and cursed his dumb, deaf wife who hadn't remembered to do the washing the day before. He didn't forget to blame himself, either, for trying to distract himself by going out into the street and failing to realise that even the simplest of his desires would lead only to disaster and ruin.

He did not have to wait in line for long before word began to spread, and by noon it was known everywhere in town, the finest and most important news of the day. So he gained yet another of his many nicknames: Sufi Urea.

And still he had no idea of the fate that awaited him.

Being a delivery boy didn't require capital; the only investment was the strength and health of one's body. So even though Alo had once said he would never do it again, he now thought to return to his former profession. He wouldn't give up when he heard the other delivery boys' comments; this was just the way things went among

|83|

them, and insults didn't matter much. Rather, one had to respond with laughter and refrain from showing anxiousness or irritability, as it didn't become a delivery boy.

It was difficult for him. He had flown high in the world of capital and wealth, but his grand dream had collapsed and forced him to come crashing down, so that he sank once again into a sweaty daily toil. From the start, he was viewed with suspicion, left without friends or companions. The remarks and insults didn't stop coming, and, more than this, he was subjected to every possible form of insolence, such as the use of his new nicknames in his presence, and even calling him by them: Sufi Urea, Sufi Bifazo. Though Urea, in the end, couldn't really stand up to Bifazo, which became the most famous, overtakking the name by which he had formerly been known, Sufi Ali Serxeti, so much so that Bifazo now stood alone, and no one bothered even to call him Sufi any longer.

Alo was, at first, annoyed by this nickname, and he complained about its popularity. But he soon realised that his annoyance only made it spread the more, and so he shut up about it, no longer complaining. In time, he grew used to it, and even came to introduce himself as Bifazo. He thought it was, at least, more local and more specific to him than Urea, which he thought was a name widespread among the unbelievers.

In the end, Sufi Ali Serxeti met his end when he fell from a pile of grain sacks that had been stacked on the bed of a truck. It was but a moment of distraction and carelessness: the truck drove into a hole that the driver didn't see, and Sufi Alo was thrown off, crushed and shredded under the rear wheels.

His death marked the end of his suffering, and the start of Hawar's.

Chapter 13

They were all so used to calling him Teacher that they forgot his real name, and Teacher became the name he was known by, even after others called teachers also came along.

Alo had asked Teacher to name his firstborn son, and he had chosen the name Hawar. At the time, he'd told Alo: "I have a good feeling about him." He then repeated this, once Hawar could understand him: "I still have a good feeling about you, and about your name, for you are the rallying cry breaking our appalling silence, a ray of hope against our overwhelming despair, the certainty to dispel our paralysing confusion."

Though Hawar wasn't able to fully comprehend what Teacher had ascribed to him, he did realise he was saying something important. He might have understood it better later, when he was running Teacher's words through his head - the words Teacher had spoken when they were both convinced they were talking past each other. Teacher was certain that Hawar would be able to appreciate what he had to say about various aspects of life, if only he would think things through. "If he can do it," he told himself, "then he deserves the life that I hope he can have, and he will be able to represent and create only what is desirable. But if he's not able to do it, then my words were in vain - like the words of many others like me, and indeed many greater than me."

Teacher taught Hawar many things, about things and events and people. He told him the life stories of everyone Hawar knew, and countless others he didn't. This was to educate him about the society in which he lived, and the people who ruled and led it, and about others whose stories would otherwise be forgotten. He told him about his father and his uncle, too, so he would see how they were viewed by others, and not as a child views a father or an uncle; thus he sought to relieve him of the burden of family and blood, which casts a shadow that might prevent one from speaking the truth, or seeing things as they really were.

He made Hawar memorise all these things, even though he knew for certain that, at that time, he couldn't understand their true meanings. But Teacher hoped this would happen eventually, and that was what pushed him forward. "He doesn't know," he told himself, "that he will understand the truth of it later. Or so I think." Through this, he also made a judgment about himself: he saw Hawar as his intellectual descendant and held himself responsible for his education and upbringing.

Teacher spoke as if he were a religious man, though he didn't bind himself by observing the strictures of piety that stifled free thought. He would pay close attention to the feelings of others when he spoke, and would never complain of answering a question, however silly or provocative. He spoke politely, which made him agreeable to everyone. Even those who didn't fully agree with him respected him: he didn't defend his views too fiercely, but rather expressed them gently, without softening them. His words were unrehearsed and simple to understand, and he didn't criticize others. He had sympathy for everyone and would give advice without hurting people's feelings. He would take care to express sound advice when he was asked to give it, and those who consulted him usually followed it, because they trusted him, his experience, and his wisdom.

"Oh, my brothers," he would say at the end of each of his gatherings. "We are all victims, we are all victims. The day will come."

Everyone would provide their own interpretation of these words; but Teacher would never comment on these interpretations directly. "Surely, it will come," was all he would say.

Teacher spoke often to Hawar about those who specialised in flattering every newcomer and those who tended to blindly follow every new trend. In an earlier era, they would have first been Frenchified, and then Turkified. They would have bent their tongues and contorted their mouths to speak in French, jabbering and raving like lunatics. But even French would not help them if they were genuinely idiots. They lived through these contradictions, with split loyalties and split identities, waiting for whomever would come to rule next so they could grovel at their feet. For some time, you would see them in the shape of communists, wearing nothing but red and speaking only to deny God. Then they adapted: they praised one leader for a time, and then turned to another, then back to the first, until they became completely confused as to who to support and who to oppose. When Nasser came along, he became their object of desire, and they were more Nasserist than Nasser himself. They would call his name day and night, and they glorified and deified him through their slogans. Their throats went hoarse from shouting: "Nasser, Nasser, God is great and God is Nasser." And after the Ba'ath came along, they turned against their own history, which had been all twists and turns from the start, and was full of lies and deceit and hypocrisy. They turned to praising Arabism and came out with new slogans: "I am Ba'ath, may my enemies die! Long live Ba'athism, and the lands of the Arabs are my homeland!" When you asked one of them about the speed with which they turned from Nasserism to Ba'athism, he would say: "We've pulled the ground from under their feet, and we walk with them so we can pounce upon them." God only knew what they would become tomorrow, and what excuses they would come up with to justify it.

"And don't forget, my friend," for Teacher liked to call Hawar "my friend," "that some of those who took on the positions of leaders, or were installed into these positions, had previously been collaborators of the French. And, before them, the Ottomans. The occupiers would reward their followers and henchmen, and they used them against whoever wouldn't comply. Today, there is a new class that's taking shape, whose policy is to honour the servile and to abase the honourable, so they can push the honourable from their homelands and make them homeless. Just wait, my friend, and you will see."

Hawar understood some of what Teacher was saying, but not all. Though, as always, he listened to him with interest and enjoyed his company.

Hawar's life went on through its proper stages, apart from a few unexpected events that ultimately changed the course of his life, as well as the lives of others.

This included Teacher. The event that changed his life forever left him nervous and anxious for a number of days, upsetting him in a very fundamental way.

He was at the national hospital in Qamishli to visit one of his acquaintances, who was on his deathbed after he had fallen off his mule. On the bus on his way back, he sat alone: he'd reserved one of the single seats, so he wouldn't annoy anyone or be annoyed by them. He chose the third row, so he would be well away from the commotion of people getting on and off the bus.

He sat in his seat, waiting for the bus to depart. It was a few minutes late, even though there were about a dozen passengers standing, and the driver had asked them all to squeeze together at the back. Then a well-built young man came on: his movements were quick, his hair was blond, and his skin fair. He took a good look at every person on the bus, examining them in turn. Then he said:

"Hey, you. Get up."

At first, Teacher pretended not to hear. But the young man wasn't happy; grabbed him by his jacket, and shook him violently. "Hey, you!" he cried, in a wild, deep voice that didn't match his graceful build at all. "Are you blind or are you deaf? Get up, right now!"

"Why would I get up from my seat?" Teacher asked. He kept his voice calm; he didn't want to lose his spot.

"What do you mean, why? Because I want you to get up, that's why!"

"There are people standing. There's no priority."

"You're no better than anyone else. Get up." He tried to drag him out of his seat.

The other passengers watched the scene in silence. Nobody dared interfere. They averted their eyes, as if they had been paralysed by fear, whoever they were and wherever they were headed. But Teacher still wouldn't budge. So the man grabbed his arm, pulled him by the sleeve of his jacket, then suddenly smashed his right hand right into his face, so that Teacher's head slammed against the window.

Blood flowed from his forehead down to his cheek. But the bigger wound was to his spirit, his dignity. He'd been completely humiliated, and his intelligence and common sense had been insulted. His clothes were stained, his eyes were overflowing with tears and blood. The world was flooded in a painful silence. Blood flowed out of every hole in his head, mixed with his flowing tears, every word and every meaning tangling together in his head.

When the driver noticed how badly the situation had deteriorated, he stepped up to the young man and coaxed him, with smiles and kind words, to take up a seat at the back, next to one of the female college students. It was, inexplicably, as if he had been the victim, and Teacher the aggressor.

In Teacher's eyes, everything had come crashing down. The humiliation and insult he felt was overwhelming. Later, many people would tell him that his stance was courageous; some would even use the word heroic. But Teacher was the only one who really knew what had befallen him, and he decided to do what he could to expose the thugs for what they were.

Silence reigned, broken only by the rumble and whir of the engine, which had been kept running. The noise helped people turn away; it whispered in their ears to ignore what had happened and seek shelter in silence. If they didn't want to suffer themselves, they should not get involved. Their daily lives were already full of humiliation, and there was no need to add to it. Little broke through the humming feelings of anxiety and abasement other than a timid request from this or that passenger to be let off in this or that village. Some avoided speaking altogether by knocking once or twice on the roof of the bus. The driver could see them in the mirror and would respond by nodding his head to signal that he understood.

News of the incident soon common knowledge throughout town,

having spread quickly from house to house. People would convey it with some exaggeration at first, shaking their shirts between their thumb and index fingers. Then they would say that this was exactly how they had heard it from someone else, trying to absolve themselves of responsibility for it, hoping it would be proven wrong. Their great admiration for Teacher couldn't allow for it, and they were shamed by associating an insult of that magnitude with the Teacher whom everyone valued and respected. Soon enough, however, others would come and confirm the news, providing more details. They would not forget, of course, to praise God's greatness and ask for His protection from the accursed Satan, who had somehow taken possession of Teacher at that crucial moment and prevented him from seeing the truth of the matter.

Teacher tried to overcome the humiliation that he felt. It would have consumed him, had he not pulled himself together and begun an open campaign of discreditation. He resorted to talking openly and critically about the outrageous, criminal behaviour of the thugs of the secret police. He cursed their leaders more than once.

He didn't pay any attention to the warnings he received. His pain was greater than anything else. Soon after, word spread that he had disappeared. Some said he had fled; others that he was in hiding; still others, that he'd been arrested. Rumours and predictions proliferated, but the only certain thing was that Teacher had disappeared, both from the town and from Hawar's life.

Hawar didn't know for sure, and really didn't want to know, whether it was the punch in the face that had made Teacher lose all hope, released his pent-up rage, and driven him toward this premature revolt, or whether it was the onlookers' silence.

One of his neighbours claimed that a patrol drove over in a jeep one morning, for a dawn raid on his house. They blindfolded him and drove him to who knows were. Afterward, the men subjected him to a few more of their select insults and punches, and then they tortured him.

Some people made predictions about the charges that would be fabricated against Teacher, leaked by those close to the secret police. They would be enough for hundreds of years of prison or several death penalties: collaborating with foreign secret agencies to take over parts of the country and annex them to a different country; complicity in crimes that led to the loss of dozens of lives; heading up an illicit intelligence network; pimping, procuring, smuggling, and theft on top of that.

Days passed, and the people forced themselves to forget about Teacher. They avoided mentioning him, in fear of being associated with him. If conversation somehow turned in his direction, the subject was quickly changed, or the gathering dissolved altogether. A mournful silence spread. People would console themselves, praising their Lord that they had not descended into recklessness like the Teacher, who did not appreciate the consequences of his words or actions.

But Hawar could not rid himself of Teacher's constant presence. He would repeat all his words to himself, as if he had recorded them and was now playing them back over and over. And he could not get over his feelings of bereavement, of becoming an orphan all over again.

What Teacher had warned of did come to pass. The day did come. But it was worse than he could ever have imagined.

Chapter 14

Hawar excelled in his studies, but he was not the kind of boy who would join his peers in their games and other activities. He was perfectly content studying and revising his lessons. Later, he would begin his explorations: he would wander around, ignoring his grandmother's constant warnings not to go too far from the house. He was stubborn and would do whatever came into his head. Unlike other children at his age, he was very much affected by the concerns of the household. He knew the meaning of poverty—he lived it and he understood it. He wanted to participate, in whatever small way he could, in meeting the household's needs, or in obtaining what he needed for himself. So, for a while, he became proficient at searching through rubbish and collecting scrap copper and aluminium, which he would then sell after he had gathered enough of it. He wouldn't bother with plastic, because, compared to other materials, the price was too low, and it would take a lot of time and effort without much reward. He much preferred metals. The scraps were smaller and lighter, and the price was better. He would melt the isolating plastic coating from discarded electric cables, then roll up the copper wires that remained until he had a ball, which could be easily stored and brought him a tidy sum. He began to distinguish between different rubbish heaps; he wasn't the only child engaged in this work, as there were others who collected more than him and with much greater skill. This was before rubbish collecting became a profession to which many families were forced to turn: newcomers to cities would have to drop their desire to leave rubbish behind and sift through the heaps in the night in silence. Eventually, they would become used to it, and would no longer feel pained or humiliated by this work; it would become a profession like other professions, officially recognised and subject to competition. They would compete over influence in particular areas, then for specific heaps, with inordinate sums spent to guarantee that they could extract whatever forgotten treasures they could, which had been thrown away out of arrogance, or stupidity.

Hawar would roll up the copper wire around a small piece of metal, originally the spout for a jug that had been used for ablutions, or maybe general washing and grooming. With every twist of the wire, his dream grew larger. He imagined different types of food, and clothes, and whatever else he thought his family might need. But, as usual, he was shocked when the scrap merchant offered to buy his metal for a meagre sum. He usually accepted what was given to him; but this time, he complained. The merchant scolded him, telling him how much work he would have to put in to thread apart the wire, as he was pretty sure that, underneath it, Hawar had hidden a piece of iron that would make the ball heavier, to try to cheat him and double the price of the scrap. He also had to fob off the officers who were pressing him to tell them about the boys who stole cables from electricity poles and tried to sell them on to him. And despite all this, he had honoured him with a pound and a half, even though it wasn't worth more than a pound and thirty-five piastres, and he'd done so only because he was a regular, and a hard-working boy that knew the job well.

Hawar was pretty sure that "Fart Ass," which was his most widespread nickname, better known than any other, wasn't an accurate description. But he seemed to have no choice but to accept it. It was as if all his dreams had been thrown aside and squashed against a wall: the paltry sum he'd been offered, the veiled threat of police, and the merchant's pretence at generosity for giving him those extra piastres. It wasn't common any longer to deal in piastres at all, except in the mind of the *kharyoun,* or the cowardly idiot, as Hawar called him in his head.

As time passed, and he gained experience, Hawar became privy to all the secrets of rubbish gathering. He could guess which area of the city a piece had come from, and even the exact house, from which he could deduce the psychological features of its owners. There were those who threw away pots that were still perfectly usable, or plastic containers that had only a hole on one side, or a cracked edge. There were those who threw away pots for tea and coffee just because they were bent or dented, or where a piece had broken off the plastic handle because of heat, or maybe just because they got bored of how the pot looked. Hawar learned to be selective, and he picked out what could be used at home, or what was otherwise useful: sturdy tools that never wore out, like different kinds of screwdrivers and pincers. These, he would bring home and boil in water mixed with lemon juice. He left things to boil for a long time, so as to get rid of the smells and dirt that clung to them.

He also began to give more importance to plastic. He would stack pieces of plastic in a corner of one of the heaps that he frequented, and when he had enough to fetch him a few pounds, he'd set aside some time to gather them up. After that, he began a final process of selection. He would create a small mound of plastic, composed of jugs, buckets, plates and other utensils, as well as tubes and hoses, including those used for farming. Then he would take them, a few at a time, to the kharyoun, who would always try to cheat him, though he would show him favour as well.

Whenever Hawar saw an opportunity, he went for it. He benefited greatly from the spring floods of the Khinzir River: the flood would clear the river channel of all that stood in its path and then discharge it on its banks, or carry it far out of town to leave it lying forgotten in the silt and sand. There was a lot of straw and plastic bags, and pieces of cardboard that seemed to be of no use. Hawar's first task, after the flood, was to comb the debris for the kinds of tools and materials that he liked to gather. He might also come across pieces of ceramic that were part of the flood's plunder from the riverside houses as it swept through in its roaring madness, or he might make even older finds that came from the ancient sites that it passed through, such as Dare, which, according to rumour, was built over gold mines.

His second task was, like that of many families, to collect the sand that the flood left behind in the wadi. The sand was useful for a number of domestic tasks, such as building roofs and floors, and filling gaps in them. Hawar wouldn't gather enormous amounts of the sand, but he managed to carry enough to create a path to the door of the house, and from the bedroom door to the courtyard. He put down the stones, one next to the other, then sprinkled the sand so it filled the gaps between them. Then he borrowed a stone roller, which was basically a stone cylinder with a hole through it for a metal chain or a rope or an iron wire. This allowed it to be pulled behind or pushed with your feet as it pressed down and smoothed and compacted a floor, or shaped a clay roof that needed regular compacting and strengthening.

Khatoune would later forbid Hawar to dig and rummage through the river debris. She feared a repeat of the disaster that had struck the town once before and took the life of Hamid al-Nouri's son. The boy had been passionate about repairing electric devices: he would search everywhere for them, despite his father's constant scolding. He would break everything that he touched when he played with it and fingered it, as his father would say when he was angry with him. It was clear that doing it to a small radio wasn't enough, and that this didn't quench the boy's thirst for more. So, like others, young Nouri would dig through the rubbish that the river disgorged on its banks. Once he happened upon a small, heavy object, which he didn't recognise at first. He set out to disassemble it ... and it exploded in his face. It was a landmine, washed up by the river from the minefields at the border.

After this incident, rumours spread that the Turks were intentionally dropping mines into the river, so they would blow up whoever was dumb enough to play around with them. People told another story about someone who got blown up by a mine in Qamishli, and then yet more stories about mines exploding, from all the towns and villages along the border. Others objected, saying that mines wouldn't just explode by themselves: they're not set on a timer, and they never stopped working, so surely it was just idiots messing around with them, idiots who didn't appreciate that the landmines were merely the cost of peace and security for this border region.

Hawar was much concerned about all this. He was forbidden from exploring the banks of the river, so he became more prudent and careful in digging through the rubbish heaps that he was familiar with, where knew every corner and could recognise every useful thing that appeared on them.

But Hawar failed to understand that he was carrying burdens that could crack his tender spine, burdens that would break the backs of men much stronger than him. He didn't realise that he was born a father, without choosing or asking for this.

He would remember what Teacher had told him about the men who were born orphans or bastards, but then grew up to lead and rule. But he didn't want to become one of them, or to follow their example. Teacher always ended up speaking most disparagingly of them; they became arrogant tyrants who sought to avenge themselves on everyone, and to absolve themselves of their past by destroying it and everyone who did or could remember it.

He didn't know, and he wouldn't know, that those who lived in poverty and experienced a change in circumstances could be considered great and powerful if they showed compassion to others. And he wouldn't think about the possibility that all had already been decided, the roles cast and the script written, and there was nothing to do but act it out.

It was enough for him to simply survive. His life, after all, was all that he had, and all that had been given to him.

Chapter 15

Grandma Khatoune was a woman wrapped in secrets. Her spirit had been honed by her homeless wanderings. Her widowhood strengthened her, and she grew wise with experience. So after her hopes had been crushed and she had lost her first-born Alo, she became convinced that she had no choice but to search for her other son, Ahme, and get him to return home, if she could do so. She'd heard that he had settled in Qarashike, and worked there as the village mullah after the old mullah had died and entrusted him his only daughter's hand in marriage, having left Ahme everything he'd owned: his honourable job, his home, his daughter, his herd, his chickens, and a sum of money that stayed in the care of his daughter, who was in charge of all household affairs.

But before she spoke with her son, Khatoune first had to turn to someone whose favour she could never forget: the woman who had sheltered her and her sons, protecting her from the ignominy that could easily have befallen her. She had saved Khatoune from the hunger whose jaws did not spare any of its victims. That woman was, to her, closer than a sister and more than a friend. She had taken her in without making her feel as though she was doing her a favour, and never accepted anything less than her fair share in any work that they undertook together. And, despite the interpretations of some of the villagers, she didn't charge her with punitive service in exchange for lodging and sympathy.

She wasn't even sure whether Perishane was still alive. She decided not to ask about her, as she would know whether she was there as soon as she approached the village. Her feelings didn't lie, nor did they trick her thoughts.

She had a look in the village cemetery and soon found the site that Perishane had chosen for her grave, next to her mother's. It was still empty. She had repeated many times that it was where she wanted to be buried, so that everyone would hear about it, in case her husband forgot.

After she had made sure that her friend was still alive, Khatoune went into her courtyard and approached the door of the house.

"Do the people of Dare still use wooden spoons?" she shouted. "Or have their spoons all turned to gold?"

Khatoune wanted to set a lighter tone for their reunion, to make it less intimidating. For her, reunions were just as painful as partings: reunions were the beginning of pain, while partings continued it and made it endless. Both meetings and partings were painful, and her life had always teetered between the two. But she had never lost the ability to smile, despite her many troubles that never seemed to ease. Her strong will, as well as her refusal to submit to her misfortunes, had helped her get used to sorrow, and sometimes even to subdue it.

"Seeing you after all these years is like finding gold! Welcome, my sister, welcome. I thought you must have forgotten us!"

Grandma Perishane could never fail to recognise the voice of her friend Khatoune, despite the weakness that had beset her sight and hearing. She didn't need to ask a second time. She tried to rise from her bed, where her ailments had been keeping her for a number of years—yet despite her infirmity, she still commanded the same respect and esteem as she always had.

"I've refused to die," she went on, with a smile, "until you could come to wash my body. Today, at least, would be a good day to die."

"God keep death away from you, and from us, and from everyone living, my sister! Today is a day for joy! We shouldn't be talking about death."

They shared a tearful hug, which wet the eyes and softened the hearts of all who were watching.

Perishane, wife of Hajj Firman al-Dari, promised Grandma Khatoune what she had promised her before: that she would be her guest for as long as she stayed in the village. This visit was the nicest gift she had received for many years, as she would greatly enjoy her time with Khatoune, sharing the good memories from the past when they had both been strong women, holding their own against the world: they had risen every morning at dawn, then kept constantly busy until they went to bed. They carried endless burdens, yet they were both content with their lives.

The village herdsman would take the flock out to the pastures; and then they began the true battle with the impossible. Each of them had to work as much as multiple women, without complaining or crying over her situation. That was just how it was. Kneading, baking, milking, cooking, cleaning, receiving guests: these and other tasks never seemed to end. This was the lot of women; and that of men was no less, if not more miserable and exhausting. Despite this, it was impossible to erase from people's minds the memory of the lives that they lived. Each of them would take on the work of many; they would perform jobs that would require the efforts of an entire team, and they would be happy and content, and indeed could not be otherwise.

So Khatoune would recount the story of the past that had never really left her memory. Decades before, she had stayed for a number of weeks in the village of Dare, as a guest of Perishane's. After that, she went to Qarashike, hoping that from there she could head toward Mardin, and from there further west, where she could lose herself in the throngs of scattered villages, clinging to her silence and ruin.

This time, it was different. The intensity of spirit that had strengthened her body had calmed, all but dying down. She was also accompanied by a grandson, fleeing with him from her loss - just as she had fled before with her sons, for a similar reason, but in the opposite direction. Time had not yet betrayed her then, as it was starting to now, spurred on by those who were waiting to ambush her; they feared that, when roles were reversed, they would be stripped naked, revealing their shortcomings, and colouring them with the shame that befit them - as they did not think, or seek advice.

"Back then, we were always busy with something," Perishane said, with a sigh. "But now, we are in this deadly stillness that can only be stirred by death."

"Our work helped us to live happily," Grandma Khatoune replied, "and to overcome the problems and misfortunes that stood in our way."

"Pasho has grown old now," Perishane whispered to Khatoune, with a mischievous smile. "But he hasn't forgotten you! He still talks about you, grumbling that you didn't say yes to him."

Her words brought back a time that was both beautiful and miserable, when joy was always blended with a good measure of sorrow, such that you couldn't distinguish between the two.

"God forgive you, sister!" Khatoune said sharply. "Haven't you forgotten that?"

She spoke harshly, but only because she so clearly recalled the time when Pasho had broached the subject, using Perishane as an intermediary. He had said that he would also provide for her sons, swearing that they would be like his own children. Her aggrieved voice was shot through with pain from a wound that could not be healed by what had passed, asking for the reason why she would choose for herself the greatest trial she had ever suffered in her life.

They both longed for their lost vitality. Old age had caught up with them and made complaints their main activity, along with great skill in recalling how things once were. Perishane, who was all but paralysed by her ailments, and Khatoune, who was all but paralysed by despair: they had both submitted themselves to desires that they would pay their entire lives to realise. But, in this place, desires had good form in not being fulfilled. It was much more common for dreams to be shattered and treatment to be sought for hearts that had been broken with sorrow. Work, work and nothing else was what filled people's lives, and especially those of women: they were pledged to service and work and childbearing, without a voice in this or value beyond it. This was not seen as patriarchy, but rather the harsh nature of life in the village, which had to be rough and inhospitable due to the ruggedness of its geography.

Khatoune began to speak of what she had to do. And while she said it to Perishane, it was as if she was telling herself:

"First, I must prepare myself to visit Sheikh Latane. Yes. Before I go to see my son, sister, I have a vow to fulfil for Sheikh Latane. I have to head to him to give him his due, and to ask him forgiveness for my tardiness in visiting him and seeking blessing from his most pure shrine. Then I will ask him to intercede, and I'll ask him to do what he can for me. He never fails to do right by his supplicants, and always heals their hearts."

She then called for the children to get her Hawar, whom she had forgotten about. When they brought him, she hurried to fuss over him, kissing and hugging him. After she had satisfied herself that all was well with him, she said:

"You have to rest now. Later we'll go to Latane's shrine, to pray for everyone."

"But Mother, I want to walk around the village a bit with Jano."

"That's fine. But don't go far. We're going to the shrine later."

"Mother, isn't a shrine like a grave?"

"So it is, my dearest."

"So, then... don't we have to pray for the dead so that God forgives them, Mother? Or do we pray to them so that they can pray for us and help us?"

"Well, my son, we pray for some of the dead, and a very few of those we pray to, it's so that they can pray for us. That's because they're saints, and God will never refuse one of their requests."

"But does God answer someone else's prayers for you?"

His grandmother scolded him, asking forgiveness for him. She didn't want to enter into an argument that she'd never thought she would have to face, and she likewise knew that she had no better answers to Hawar's innocent questions.

Once their conversation had ended, Hawar went to the door to look over the village, and to think about what he'd just talked about with his grandmother. The silence was broken by a muffled cry from Perishane: through the window, she had just seen Pasho approaching the house. She smiled and winked at Khatoune, in a way that did not befit her age at all:

"Pasho's coming, sister! He hasn't stopped thinking about you for a single day. And he's still repeating the same things he always had, that he'd been saying to himself and to everyone, so that they would console him. 'Oh, I swear that she's the most beautiful of all the girls! I swear she looks like she's never conceived or born a child!"

People didn't quite know what to say to him, so they kept away, and they wondered.

Khatoune was happy, at least, that Pasho had cut off Hawar's embarrassing questions. "He's very welcome," she said. "He's always been like a brother to me. I respect him a lot."

When Hawar realised that Pasho was the old man who was approaching the house, he hurried to him so that he could help the man ascend; both Perishane and his grandmother didn't hesitate in asking him for this, especially because Pasho had been losing his balance recently.

Hawar was greatly upset by the disagreement that was later to emerge between himself and Grandfather Pasho, for they each had completely different things on their minds. He hurried over to support the old man and to help him ascend the stone steps in front of the house. He had been raised to respect his elders: he would call everyone who was older than him Uncle, or Grandfather, like his mother had taught him. In turn, Pasho was very glad to see the reverence in the boy's eyes, and how quick he was to kiss his hand. But his gladness evaporated when the boy grabbed his hand and started pulling him forward, saying:

"Give me your hand, Grandfather, so you don't fall down the steps!"

Hawar said it sincerely and innocently; he only expressed what he thought was his duty, and wanted nothing but to help. But Pasho thought that the child's hurry to help him was so he could sit in his lap and get something from him. Usually, children would curry favour so they could get some sweets, or some money; this was the price for helping him. And it would make them happier than if they'd received more from somebody else. Grandpa Pasho's money had a different and sweeter flavour to it.

"Don't tell me to get up there, son. You're still a strong, young man. Or will you carry me with you? You've come to warn me of falling, and other misfortunes. So you won't get your tip from me today, Jano."

He'd smiled when he heard the slight tone of doubt in the young man's voice. Obviously the young man had been brought up according to values that enjoined him not to lie, or to contradict those whom he respected. Pasho was glad to realise this, and he tried to comfort himself further by recalling some of the happiest days of his own life, when he was roaming carefree through the plains and valleys, day and night, foraging and wandering.

"I'm not Jano, Grandfather, I'm Hawar. Or do you want me to lie to you, Grandfather?"

Hawar said it respectfully, though with some annoyance; but it was well tempered, as he didn't want to go against what he'd been taught. He was innocent and sincere, and unaware of the silent balance between the tip that awaited him when Grandfather would arrive in his seat, and the need to lie. For if his parents had ever learned that he had lied, they brought all their anger to bear upon him. They had always told him: son, don't lie, always tell the truth, even if you're on the gallows. So the boy had duly remembered all the sayings and proverbs that exhorted him to tell the truth, and condemned lying, and classified it all as a most heinous crime, without distinguishing between good lies and bad lies. They were all called lies, and they were all bad. One might claim to do good things by lying; but in the end, it caused only ruin, and no attempt at renaming or embellishing it could rectify that.

"I want you to speak nicely to me, son. But whose son are you, Hawar?"

Pasho now sought to somehow fix the mess that he'd waded into. He'd been carried away by his desire to preserve the traces of his youthfulness, which had long been dwindling. It had seeded dreams in his mind and burdened him with regrets, as he lost himself in measuring what his life had been against what was and what would be. He imagined himself as the fearless boy and then the strong youth that he'd been, and other events that played out before his eyes without ever reaching the stage of life that he was living now, which was so far from the beauty and perfection that he remembered. He didn't want to make the boy feel that he'd done something wrong or that he was overly hasty in offering to help him, when he tried, with an old man's wickedness, to distract him and chide him with his words. He didn't want to be blamed that he'd asked the boy to deceive - or, really, to lie - or to make him feel guilty for his appraisal of an old man. It was his due, after all, to teach the younger generations to tell the truth, and to be honest in their words and actions.

"I'm the son of my mother Khatoune," Hawar told him. And before he could think about what he'd just said, he quickly added: "So come up the stairs on your own then, Grandfather. You're still strong!"

He couldn't quite understand why the old man was refusing to acknowledge the truth. He seemed intent on making others feel as though they were at fault and that they were mistreating him, accusing them of having changed their behaviour, and deriding their reverence toward him. All of this was going through Hawar's head, without really understanding why, or being able to put his thoughts into words, and it only contributed to the feelings of accusation and blame that lingered between them.

When he heard Khatoune's name, Pasho was struck, as though a shooting star had fallen on him from the sky: it revived the memory of the beauty that had once so overwhelmed him and made him quite unjustly disposed towards the woman who had possessed it. "You are a dear brother," she'd told him, "but the woman that I once was is no more. I'm now a mother of two children, and there's no space for anything else in my life." But though he knew that Khatoune was coming, he still clung to the thought that what he was hearing was but a dream; for it was only dreams that could bring back the Khatoune that had taken over his heart and his spirit without ever intending it.

"You're being a little harsh, son."

Pasho tried to ignore that he'd been called Grandfather and sought to strike back at the boy who appeared to him just then to be a fierce opponent, with clever justifications for his own thoughts and actions. So he moved their conversation toward accusations: he charged the boy with what he feared most—that he was belittling his capabilities—or, indeed, that he had only hurried toward him in order to get some money. He thus turned his near defeat into a sudden counter-attack that his opponent wasn't expecting. He knew it wasn't justified, and indeed harsh to do so, but his fear of accepting the truth had made it necessary for him to improvise his response. He was convinced that the boy would accept defeat, merely out of respect, as well as his unwillingness to contradict him.

"Grandfather, I swear, I'm just trying to help."

It seemed as if he were now committed to the path that the old man had led him onto. He'd made him doubt his upbringing, and the man might as well have called him rude. He had no choice but to defend himself from the old man's accusation, to say that he was afraid for his welfare.

As their battle of words went on, they reached the top of the stairs, the old man leaning on the boy, claiming that he didn't want it, even while the boy served as a second walking stick in addition to the one that he was holding and waving in the air, as he bumped against him with every step.. Their quarrel finished with each accusing the other, in his mind.

He does resemble the love that took my happiness from me, so long ago. And like my heart, he will never understand . . .

The old man's crazy.

What is wrong with me?

It's my fault for trying to help him.

He's a naughty boy... His heart wouldn't let him call the boy rude.

What can I do? It seems he's old and stupid.

It's better to die than reach feeble old age, and to suffer at the hands of these kids.

God take me before I ever help this crazy old man again!

I won't give him money and I won't give him sweets, either!

What will he give me? I've no idea.

Khatoune and Perishane watched from the window as the quarrel between Pasho and Hawar deepened.

"May God protect Hawar for me," Khatoune muttered to herself, with a smile, "and God give me patience for him."

When they approached the door, she greeted Pasho and welcomed him. Though she spoke to only one of them, they each thought her words were directed to the other, as they weren't looking at her eyes when she spoke; though even if they had, it wouldn't have helped, because she was looking at the ground:

"Don't you know that we're the most annoyed with those that we love!"

Chapter 16

Dare, from the south, looked like a throne, though there was no monarch seated on it. From the north, from the mountain plateau against which it rested, it looked like an open hand, speckled with little hills of various sizes. But from within, it blinded you with the misery of what you saw, images that did not match the kindness of the people that fell under your scrutinising gaze.

Dare was composed of four parts: Agha in the south, Hajiya in the east, Kalahih in the the north, and in the west the Falla, or the Christian quarter. The latter was an ancient name; no Christians lived there now. But the rulers of Dare had once been Christian, before the Muslims came and imposed their laws upon it. It thus represented an example of the kind of ethnic mixing that improved the reputation of a place and was wholly unconcerned with its history - which nobody worried about anyway, whether it was good or bad.

There was constant strife between the four parts of Dare. The people of each part thought themselves the only legitimate inhabitants and sought to keep everything for themselves. A minor dispute over water for irrigation could lead to a person's death; and a number of people were killed in an argument over some straw. In the end, the real victim was the village itself, which lost its social cohesion, and the enmity and aggression that simmered in it led to its gradual obliteration.

A visitor to Dare would find, in every house, that an old sock had been hung from the ceiling in one of the rooms. The sock would be filled with coins, as well as bits and pieces of other antique rubbish that the people of the house might find and later try to find some use for. The villagers would wait until the heavens blessed them with rain, and after the rainwater had washed away the top layer of soil, they would set out to gather ancient artefacts. The rain cleaned the face of the earth, and in so doing, showed them its generosity. It revived their pastures and reinvigorated their spirits, so they walked happily around the village, their heads never far from the ground, looking for an artefact or antique that might contribute to their livelihood or provide their families with something that they needed. Another of the Darian customs was, therefore, to constantly pray for rain, because rain brought them many benefits, more than it brought to the inhabitants of the villages around them.

Dare was the village of prohibitions. Digging, building, renovating, and demolition were all among the forbidden activities. And yet there were always fools who would dig or destroy or dismantle without rebuilding, or discover without publicising once's discovery, and so deepen the divisions between the four parts of Dare, until they destroyed and broke its final stone. This encouraged the people of the village to hasten its destruction; it was a danger that should have been avoided, for it fed the fires of division, and created one dispute after another, with no time between them to look for a solution. The endless disputes also crossed over into the affairs of the young: who was meant to be with whom, and who wasn't, drawing the lines for their futures, linking the names of some to others who had been chosen for them. And if anyone dared to refuse, both sides would pay the price. The dispute would escalate into irrigation rights, and then to pastures and herd animals and chickens, and perhaps even to the sky itself... So the villagers would always look for something to fight over, to keep the flames of their disputes blazing, intensifying day after day. Nobody wanted to subject themselves to the trouble of soul-searching or self-reflection, for that might jeopardise one's standing and prestige, which were propped up so weakly in the midst of a land with no compassion, one that was bursting with thorns and poison.

There was little that exceeded the villagers' hate for each other, except their hatred for the Turkish military that had, somehow, insinuated itself among them. They would say to each other: "The vultures here are pretending to be eagles" or, "the cats here pretend to be lions." The guard post had been installed close to the square that connected all four parts of Dare, where the city's hills met. It ruined their lives, and they complained about the post whenever they passed it. They hated it because it forbade them their right to secure their futures and the futures of their children. It forbade them any sort of real work and made them into prisoners in caves that they'd been forced to turn into dwellings, or places where they could hide their beloved when they committed their sins. The tombs became the barns and troughs for their cattle, or places to stack their supplies and animal feed. It looked down at them, watchful and untiring, preventing them for realising their hopes and dreams, and viciously suppressing any attempt at doing so. It showed no mercy.

Chapter 17

In the stony, stubborn village of Dare, the plains met the mountains, and the ancient past met the living present. It bore witness to an uneffaceable history, a subject of neglect and disregard, and was a victim of a poisoned blade that forever divided it. It was guarded by its name, that of King Darius, and time was witness to the fact that even he was unable to destroy it, because it could never be destroyed.

In the company of Jano, the grandson of their host, Hawar liberated himself from the instructions and advice that his grandmother and his parents had imposed upon him all his life. Now he found himself free, unbound by any rules. His grandmother was preoccupied with their host and had entered with her into a seemingly endless conversation about the glories of the past, as well as its injustices: how time would bring people success, only to betray them later, destroying their every hope. So while his grandmother was busy, Hawar took the chance to join the village kids in their explorations, amazed by everything he saw.

It didn't take him long to realise that the village was divided into four nearly equal parts. Each part was built on a different hill, cut through nearly in half by the river that ran from Qirdis toward Amouda, from the northeast to the southwest, and in the other direction where the hills met, from the southeast to the northwest. The two lines crossed to produce the four parts of Dare, and the square, where they met, was the focal point of the village, which none of the parts could do without. The reality of geography produced a division that seemingly satisfied everyone - though in truth, it satisfied no one. The conflicts and disagreements were clearly visible, starting with the claims that the children made about particular historical sites in the village, each of which was allocated to a different one of their families.

Hawar was happy. He felt free in these mountains, breathing clean air, untroubled by the fears that usually haunted him. He never knew where to go; he believed he was an impostor, with no right to stay anywhere. His grandmother had taught both her sons, and her grandson after them, that they might be seen as bastards, but God knew that they were lords. But they had been betrayed, made strangers in their own land, outsiders in every town and village. And outsiders had to show deference and respect their boundaries, which did not apply to the native inhabitants of the place. They had no allies, and they were taught to keep away from the kind of conflicts and enmities that might burden them trouble they could ill afford. They were also taught never to get involved in any fights they might come across, as mediation required attributes that they didn't possess, and intervening would only cause them more pain, earning them the hatred of one of the sides.

They began by taking him around the entire village. He thought it took only a few moments, though in fact it was hours. They ran and played and laughed. Whenever they passed a landmark, they explained everything about it to Hawar, including the role it had played in the past.

It was strange to find a place so full of culture and history only a few kilometres from his town, a place that he'd never even heard of. He'd only known its name from the expression that people used when they criticised someone, usually a tall person who they considered stupid and worthless: "Look at him, like the Bartawil of Dare, he doesn't understand anything."

The water channel that surrounded the ancient city was engineered so that it distributed the water all around the walls, creating a moat that prevented entry. The surrounding hills had been precisely carved so that not a drop of water was held in them; their stone was steep and smooth, and they could neither be climbed nor tunnelled through. So every visitor was forced to enter through the gate, which was bounded on one side by the "Bartawil" - a giant rock - and on the other by the ruins of an ancient mill, which now served as a shelter for feral donkeys. The passage in between was paved with giant stones that were each more than three metres long, and, at regular intervals, it was studded with the remains of bases that once would have held statues that adorned the main entrance to the city. There were also guard posts positioned skillfully all around it, some with one floor and some with two, according to the height of the land on which they stood.

Hawar ran after the kids to the southeast hill of the village; they were always ahead of him, as they were very good at scaling the rocks and finding the right footholds so that they wouldn't slip. By the time he caught up, they had gathered around a huge pile of rocks; this had gaps that were big enough to stick your head in, or another rock. When he asked them what was inside, they told him that the stones had been put there to cover a bottomless well. He was astonished, and one of the kids told him to put his head in one of the gaps so he could see. He was nudged forward by his love of exploration, and his boundless curiosity; so he did it, and put his head where he was told. But it was so dark inside that he couldn't see anything, so he had to throw in a stone, and even though he listened very hard for it, he couldn't hear the sound of it hitting the bottom, or even an echo. The kids then started telling him their own theories about the well.

Some said it led into Hell, as it had swallowed children who had gone in too far when trying to uncover its secrets. Some said that it led to a city of the djinn. Others said that it led to a secret place where the king and his guard could run and hide if the city was attacked.

Hawar was impressed by all this, although what he would hear later was much stranger, and much more incredible.

The children became his guides to the city. They noticed how interested he was in anything they had to say about the history buried in the village that overlooked the ruins, although they sometimes contradicted each other, to the extent that they nearly came to blows over whether one or the other's opinion was correct.

After Hawar's tour of the village, they gathered under the wall on the northeastern side, to rest a little like he wanted to. Then they continued with the tour that they had conducted many times before, to tell visitors what they knew.

Hawar didn't interfere in the seemingly endless disputes that the children of the warring parts of Dare acted out on a daily basis. He didn't side with any of them at the expense of another; and so, in the few days he spent with them, his presence seemed to guarantee a semblance of peace. He would wander around with everyone, take a liking to everyone, and everyone would take a liking to him.

He didn't get bored of moving between the different parts of the village; on every trip, he would discover something new, and everything that he encountered amazed him greatly. Some of the kids called him stupid, or green, or ignorant—or even, sometimes, an "Arab". The latter especially implied that he was uncivilised, a barbarian from the furthermost reaches of the wilderness, naïve and uneducated.

He nearly got lost when some of his escort hurried ahead to disappear into the caves in the east of Hajiya, which were called the Barbarka; and specifically the easternmost of these caves, which they called Shakafta Daf Lihwa. Its opening was directed upward; inside, it was split into two floors, and the kids had gathered and hidden in the upper floor, so that he couldn't see any of them when he peered in through the entrance. But he laughed when he discovered their ruse, discovering there was a passage inside that led to the upper floor.

After this, they went to the river and splashed around and played in the water. Hawar was a little baffled by what he saw there. There were stone crosses on the banks of the river, where birds had sought to build their nests in safety. But the kids harassed the birds, attacking and raiding their nests to find unhatched eggs—though recently, they had eased off on this practice, after one of them had been stung by a scorpion when sticking his hand into one of the nests.

Hawar didn't even want to stop to take a breath. He was propelled by an intense desire to learn more about this ancient world that he had never imagined finding in his homeland. He urged the kids to show him what else there was to see, and he wouldn't accept any of their excuses regarding rest, or postponing the explorations of their wonderful, strange city until tomorrow. They finally relented and took him to the Christian quarter, famous for its buried riches, gemstones, and antiques. This was the centre of authority in ages past and stood as a testament to the wealth that could be found in it. They showed him the royal palace in the western part, and the tall caves that had served as additional defences for its inhabitants, and were now used as stables or storerooms, with no regard for rockfalls or natural erosion. When they passed the guard post, every single one of them spat out a curse that was much like the curses they exchanged among themselves; but here, they were coloured with hatred and protest. They curses were accompanied by gestures that implied sexual intercourse, and they pointed their sticks at the soldiers to intimidate them.

The ruins of the royal palace betrayed the great age and magnificence of a kingdom that had been once the grandest in the area. But now, it had turned into a place where kids fooled around and people stored their supplies and fed their animals, as well as a hiding place for lovers who felt constrained by the village, suffocated by its walls which could not conceal them, and overwhelmed by love that didn't care about the realities of endless work.

He had never tasted figs that were softer or sweeter than the figs he made himself sick with when he ate too much in Wadi Dare. This lay to the northwest of the village, and it grew thick with all kinds of trees, figs and olives and walnuts and almonds and oaks. A visitor could never grow tired of it: its air cleared the lungs and comforted the soul, and the valley eased your pains and sorrows in its blessed, generous vastness.

Some of the kids grew bored with Hawar and his endless questions and wanted to conclude their tour by leading him to the prison. They wanted to scare and shock him, given that he'd never seen anything like it, or even heard about it.

He entered the ancient prison of Dare through its main gate, which was about a metre in height and less than that in width. The top was fashioned in the shape of an arch; it was said that it had been discovered after someone removed a large stone to use as foundation for their house. The gate led to a horizontal passage about two metres wide and more than twenty metres long, and at its end was a stair leading downward. There were three underground floors. It was so dark inside that, at first, the prison looked small to Hawar, but the huge columns that rose through it, in groups of three, revealed its true size. Some of the walls were pierced by holes, which let in a little light to combat the thick darkness.

It was like the darkness in a forgotten tomb, and it gave the place a desolate feel. There were lanterns, but they lit up barely a metre around them, and they were at least four metres apart, fastened to columns that rose up and up to where Hawar couldn't see. It was like he'd been thrown into the well that they'd tried to frighten him with earlier. The smell of damp made him dizzy, and he almost fell to the ground, but managed to control himself, holding on to one of the kids by tugging at the bottom of his jumper.

In the depths of the underground prison, the children turned into ghosts. Their movements were soft and quiet, their eyes shone like the eyes of cats. Their shouts shook Hawar and made him tremble; he was blind, he didn't know what he was doing. The darkness lay heavy on him. The ceiling of the prison was like a night sky alight with stars, faint and flickering as if covered by sheets of dark cloud. Though at the very top, right in the centre, there was a sheaf of light that fell all the way down to the damp floor, like a spotlight on a singer trapped in a darkness from which there was no escape, and which could never be dispelled. That opening at the top was like the moon lighting up the prison's sky, dark and heavy and suffocating.

After a while, he got used to the darkness. Little by little, the dark clouds began to dissipate, and he began to distinguish the columns one from another. He looked around him and saw the decaying, crumbling walls, stripped down to the stone, and the children who were moving intently along them, searching here and there, digging under a particular pillar or step. In the corner, he saw the entrance to a small room; cautiously, he approached. A boy was digging away close to it. Hawar asked him about it, and the boy told him that it had once been a solitary cell, for holding the most dangerous criminals. Hawar entered, realising that it was circular, constructed like an inverted funnel. He touched the walls; the stones were smooth and damp, and his fingers slid across them easily. Rays of light fell from above through a hole that seemed tiny when he looked at it. When the boy found him staring closely at the walls, he told him that Hamza al-Baylawan had once escaped from this cell, when they'd imprisoned him there.

Hawar didn't believe that; the smoothness of the walls was enough to tell him that they couldn't be scaled without falling off, and they had to be more than thirty metres high. He filed it away as a legend, or a story the kids had come up with. Still, his thoughts kept coming back to it.

Jano took his hand and led him to the side of one of the pillars, where they stood together in a group. He shifted a stone and asked Hawar to stretch his neck and look inside. He then told him that a group of people had once come from one of the countries in Europe. They'd stayed in the village as guests and had a great many maps with them. Once, after midnight, they went into the prison and dug into that pillar. It was said that they took away huge quantities of gold, and many other treasures, including keys to palaces that hadn't yet been discovered.

All that he saw, and all that he heard, thrilled and amazed Hawar. When they left the prison, the light hurt his eyes, and he couldn't fully open them until they'd been above ground for some time. He felt like he'd been imprisoned in that strange solitary cell and had just now been released; he stumbled over every stone and couldn't catch his breath properly until they'd crossed the bridge that passed over the river. They then went up onto the larger, central bridge. There, he stopped, noticing that there were two parallel lines running along it. He asked what they were, but most didn't bother answering after the youngest child told him:

"This was the road for the king's carriage."

Chapter 18

After their wanderings had tired them out, the boys retreated to the mosque. This lay in the centre of the village, close to the guard post, and was supposed to bring everyone together. In the courtyard, Hawar washed his face and dribbled some water onto his head, and then he rested with his new-found friends.

"Do you see the words written on that stone?" Little Pasho asked him. "They're from long before Islam. It's in a language nobody understands now. They say that this mosque was a church once, or maybe a temple . . . but for which religion? Nobody knows."

"I think it was a church," Jano said. "You must have heard the proverb that goes: 'Even had nobody taken advice and followed the true path, the Christians of Dare would've still become Muslims.'"

The mosque was the only place in the village not subject to dispute. It represented the bond of religion that, in theory, transcended all other bonds. He would later learn that the people of Dare weren't bound together by ties of blood or kinship; they were known to have no noble who ruled over them, which was a source of great pride to many of them, as each of them was responsible for his own family and ruled over it. This may well have been a practice in its distant past, when it was a city of some size and importance wherein many families sought refuge. It also reflected its role in passing down the laws and customs of a settled civilisation, with no connection to the tribal laws that were seen elsewhere as the absolute, sacred authority.

It was said of the Darians that, if a dispute arose among them, they would never take it to a judge who would judge the case according to Islamic law, because that law undermined their right to get what they needed in their own particular ways, and they didn't want to lose what they hid from it. So the mosque remained a point of agreement between all of them, as it didn't stand for the power of any over another, and there was no adjudication there, and nobody lost anything.

The children's knowledge amazed Hawar. They knew so much about their village and cited names of Greek and Roman and Persian kings. When they fell into discussing the history of the village, they went back to pre-Christian times and knew all the dates exactly. Others would add more information about what happened later, the centuries of the Christians and the Muslims and the Ottomans, about those who helped build and restore the village that was once a flourishing capital, and about those who helped the years on their inexorable march toward destruction, until it was ruined and forgotten.

Chapter 19

Pasho insisted that his grandson be circumcised in Khatoune's arms. He wanted to strengthen the kinship ties that could only come from holding a child to be circumcised, and that sometimes transcended the ties of blood. This would mean he could call her his *karifa*, as if that could compensate from the long decades that separated them.

Khatoune was confused. She claimed that she wasn't trained to do something like that, and she begged him to spare her this task. But Pasho swore that he wouldn't be circumcised unless she agreed to hold him. Should he remain impure for the rest of his life, if he wasn't to be purified in her arms? And if he remained like an infidel, it would be her fault.

Khatoune was completely unprepared to take part in something like this, and it was now being imposed on her like it was her duty. Pasho seemed to sense this, so he added another oath, swearing that she wouldn't have to do anything else that a *karif*, or "holder", would normally need to do. He absolved her of any gifts - although he had already prepared a gift to give to Hawar.

With Khatoune, everything was different.

Perishane implored her to fulfil Pasho's wish, even though she didn't know anywhere, anywhere at all, where a boy had been circumcised in the arms of a woman. The matter usually stayed between men; the women provided the ululations and made the food.

It was clear that people treated Khatoune very much like she was a man - as if her age had stripped her of her womanhood and turned her into a man. In the end, she consented, if under duress. She knew that she was nearing the final stages of her life, and she didn't want to embarrass Pasho, or Perishane, who were both very dear to her.

Pasho seemed overjoyed and invigorated by this, and he prepared a huge celebration. Most of the villagers were invited; a number of sheep were slaughtered, and two rams. It was like the joy of a long-postponed wedding, if only in Pasho's mind.

Hawar was getting ready with the other children who were gathered outside the door to run after Little Pasho—who was the oldest grandson of Grandpa Pasho, and his namesake. The boy being circumcised was his brother. They heard a long scream, followed immediately by wailing, and accompanied by ululations and cheers and shouts of "God is great," from both men and women. Some of the men were bending their arms at the hip, as if firing a few shots into the air; but they refrained from this and only snapped their fingers, while under their breaths they cursed the government that had forbidden them to celebrate.

Pasho brought out the foreskin that had once covered the boy's penis, and which had polluted his innocence; it was said that, had it stayed in its place, it would have cursed him forever. He gave it to his grandson, who wrapped it in a piece of cloth that he'd prepared for this purpose, and then set to run away quickly. All the other kids chased after him, until they reached the Bartawil. On the southwestern side of it, where water gathered after heavy rain, he stopped, took a deep breath, and then fell down to his knees. He dug into the earth and removed some pebbles until he had made a small hole. Once his job was done, he raised his hands, laughed, and shouted:

"May God make his dick grow as big as this Bartawil!"

They all laughed with him, and then they ran back to enjoy the delicious food with their families.

Hawar was swept up in contradictory emotions: he felt very happy, and at the same time very sad. Though he was glad he'd been able to join the kids, he envied Little Pasho the joy of those moments when he was burying his brother's foreskin. He was shaken by his feelings of loneliness; he wished he had a brother, older or younger, so he could relish the gift of brotherhood and friendship between them. He'd thrown his front milk tooth onto the roof, begging the old witch to replace him with someone better than him. But when the other children did it in the company of others, it seemed natural and joyful; whereas he only felt sadder and lonelier.

"Why do they call you an orphan if you lost your mother or father? Why don't they call you an orphan if you don't have a brother? Why have I been denied this blessing? Why can't I be like them?"

The questions kept coming. But, as always, he had no answer.

Chapter 20

The shrine of Sheikh Muhammad, known as Sheikh Latane in those remote parts, lay to the northeast of Upper Qarashike, and to the northwest of Dare. It and the two villages formed one corner of an irregular triangle. To the south of the shrine was the small village of Kundike Maqso. From Amouda, it looked like a green smudge on the side of the mountain; though for the pilgrims who visited it, it was like paradise.

Among the families who lived there, it was said - and passed down and remembered through the generations - that the shrine should remain untouched, as the saint still lay in it, and that he wouldn't allow anyone to approach his resting place or take anything away that belonged to him from the surrounding land. He would avenge himself most fiercely upon anyone who committed such a crime; he possessed much power, and this needed no evidence beyond the great number of people who were struck deaf by his miracles. The stories were passed down through the generations, even though nobody could tell the exact time or place where these events had occurred.

Two incidents in particular spread his fame far and wide. Once, a fierce blaze had started in one of the village houses and burnt down all that it touched. It destroyed six whole houses and reduced them to ash. The man of the seventh house climbed onto the roof and waved his hands desperately, imploring Sheikh Latane to save him and put out the fire before it destroyed his house as well. He shouted at the top of his voice:

"Save us, oh Sheikh Latane, save us. Save my mother and save my father, save us. Help us, oh lord, help us. Show us your miracles, let us silence your enemies with them. Save us. Help us . . . save us."

Only a few moments passed before the heavens were torn apart with thunder and lightning, and rain came flooding down, putting out the fearsome blaze that had destroyed everything in its path. So the Sheikh's help brought relief in a time of great need.

The second story told of Oum Mourad. When her first child was born, the infant wouldn't feed on her breast, and so her milk dried up, and her breasts grew inflamed. All the milk slowly trickled out, and the pain it caused was intense. One of the women advised her to ask Sheikh Latane for help, before her child grew hungry and died. Oum Mourad then sought solace from the Sheikh: she sought his blessing, and she carried her child in her arms while she walked around his blessed shrine. She presented her offerings to the Sheikh and gave food to all those who passed by, pilgrims both human and djinn. After a sleepless night of desperate pleas and supplications, the mother finally lay down and slept close to the shrine in a room that had been set aside for women, with her son in her arms. She woke up after a short while, having dreamt a dream that cured her of all her ailments: the sheikh had put his hand on the infant's head and calmed him, ordering him to suck on his mother's breast; for he would be one of the true believers, and would never need anything else after her, for he had been chosen to be beloved by God, and serve his saint the good Sheikh.

To this, they added that no sooner had the mother woken up than the infant opened his mouth like a little bird begging for food. No harm ever befell him, for he'd been cured of whatever had caused him and his mother their illness, which had nearly killed them both.

Chapter 21

Wadi Dare was always green; its waters were always flowing; its pastures were always verdant, and its trees always bore fruit. It provided the best grazing, so herds of cattle stood intermingled with flocks of sheep and goats. All the herdsmen came together there: they sat and gathered, from sunrise to sunset, and sometimes they would stay in the valley overnight and converse in the light of the moon, around a fire enriched by the meat that they had pinched from the shrine, and the fruit or vegetables that came with it. The pastures weren't used only by the animals of the Darian people, but also served as common grazing for those of the neighbouring villages.

Ramko, Hawase, and Osko were three of the herdsmen who were there nearly all the time. Ramko herded the cattle of Dare; Hawase herded the cattle of Qarashike; and Osko herded the sheep that belonged to him and his uncle here and there. Osko would stay in the valley with the other two for days at a time, then go away and come back after a few days or sometimes weeks. He didn't keep to any one place, which often made his father and uncle angry with him. "You're tiring out the animals," they'd reprimand him, "by constantly moving around, you idiot."

Ramko and Hawase were always busy, not with their herds and their grazing, but rather with how to pilfer as much as possible from the offerings that had been presented to the shrine of Sheikh Latane.

Before they told each other the secret of what they had been doing to the shrine's visitors, and combined their efforts, they hadn't wanted to spoil their profits. They took what they could from the offerings at the shrine, taking advantage of the generosity of the visitors, who would, for the most part, cry and pray and present their gifts to the Sheikh. Then they would leave. Some visitors might lay down and sleep next to the Sheikh's resting place, hoping that perhaps he would visit them in a dream, and fulfil all their requests, and heal their sorrow, or cure them of their ailments.

But it was difficult for both Ramko and Hawase to keep the secret. It weighed heavily on them, for each had kept it to himself for far too long. All the time they'd spent together gave them a semblance of trust; they chatted about pretty much everything and soon realised that they agreed about many things. So they slowly disclosed their practices, after they'd made sure of their feelings about them, and revealed their intentions. Ramko spoke about the shrine and its munificence, which extended to all that surrounded it:

"God has blessed this place, and sent gifts to its people. Don't you think so, Hawase, my brother?"

In the beginning, Hawase was perhaps a little more cautious and tentative than Ramko. So Ramko didn't wait for him to respond, but merely finished the thought that was already running through Hawase's head:

"I say, my brother. Given that God has given us such a blessed place... why wouldn't we take advantage of this? Why don't we take Him up on his generosity, and thank him for his gifts?"

"Praise be to God, always," Hawase said, nodding and giving his blessing to the idea.

"So why don't we clean up around the shrine, and get our reward for it? Surely there's no harm in benefitting from God's blessings?"

In this way, Ramko touched the heart of the matter, and he touched Hawase's heart as well, as Hawase was fascinated by him, and envied his convincing arguments.

"By God, you only speak the truth. Your beautiful words are enough to make me join you in drinking the sweet milk of the mayor's cow."

He eagerly proceeded to milk the cow and filled two pans of milk for them.

They drank the milk and agreed that the matter would remain their secret. They didn't want the villagers to misunderstand their "cleaning up" the shrine, as some of them coveted even the excrement of their animals, which they might use as fertiliser or fuel. And they swore that they would share everything that the shrine might grant them through the visitors' offerings.

Still, there were misunderstandings and quarrels to get through before they'd hashed out the details of their agreement. At first, when one of them would see someone approaching, he would leave his cattle and hurry toward the shrine, with the excuse of having to relieve himself. He would then hide behind the branches of a tree, or some rocks, waiting for the visitor to leave after they'd set their donation at the shrine, hoping it might benefit a passerby, or a bird or mammal, or any of God's creatures, or perhaps even feed the Sheikh resting in the shrine.

Once, they both pounced on the same roast chicken, and it ended up rolling in the dust, just as they both did as they fought over it. This fateful fight not only ruined the chicken, but also caused their cattle to run and scatter through the valley far from their pasture, and they had to go through the misery of gathering them back together and chasing after the strays. After that, they agreed to distribute their duties clearly: one would always guard both of their cattle while the other was "cleaning up" the offerings. And through all this, they cared not one bit for the villagers and families, who would never have thought to ask themselves about the fate of the food and money that they left behind to honour the Sheikh, in the hope that he would cure them of their ills.

"The good thing about being a shepherd is that you get to fuck donkeys." This proverb implied that there might be certain perquisites that come with a job, beyond just the required tasks. But Ramko and Hawase changed it into a proverb that better suited them, and them alone: "The good thing about being a shepherd is that you get to eat chicken and lamb."

Before they began to properly take turns in their work, Osko appeared with his herd. He wore nothing but a robe of indeterminate colour, fastened with a leather belt that the years had turned almost black, though it might have started out brown. He had his stick as well, which he never stopped waving around.

He came from the direction of Mardin, where he'd been herding his sheep along the road. He was overjoyed whenever someone in a passing vehicle waved at him in greeting; he would respond at length, calling to God and repeating his words over and over:

"Peace be upon you and God's mercy and blessings, may God bring peace and good fortune to your homes, and keep your flocks safe, and bless them for you, and may God be pleased with you and with us all."

They thought about what they might say to Osko, and how to

win him over. He never could keep anything to himself; not out of wickedness, but because he wasn't able to do otherwise. So they agreed not to tell him anything, as they couldn't rely on him keeping silent, and they didn't try to ask for his support, as they knew he wouldn't be able to keep his word, and probably wouldn't even remember that he'd promised them anything. He was a simple man, easy to trick in just about anything - except his herd, and his dog, and his donkey. But apart from that, there was nothing that mattered to him.

They agreed that, in front of visitors to the shrine, one of them would claim to be entrusted with being its caretaker, or its "servant," as he would describe himself to strangers. As soon as they saw someone approaching, he would hurry along and sit himself down next to a tree or a big rock close to the shrine, and pretend to be a dervish, muttering prayers and supplications and asking God's forgiveness, only to quickly pounce upon whatever the visitor might be ready to give away, in vows or sacrifices to the spirits of their dead relatives, and the living, and the spirit of Sheikh Latane.

They gorged themselves on meat after every such visit, as the faithful were all too happy to give their offerings to the servant of the shrine so he could distribute them to the poor. Or perhaps they didn't care much about what happened to their offerings, as long as they returned with a clear conscience, believing that they had fulfilled their vows. Their sacrifice in God's name would lift the sorrow that had enveloped them ,which would not leave them until they walked around the shrine and asked for the Sheikh's blessing and intercession, so that they could be cured, or forgiven their errors and their sins. They would even ask forgiveness of the Sheikh that they had left it until so late to visit him, and they might address the stones of his grave and the dilapidated walls of his tomb regarding the consequences of what had happened to them.

Osko's presence posed something of a challenge to them, at the start. They knew what he was like: that he couldn't hold his tongue, and loved to gossip, and had no discretion about anything. They tried to convince him to stay in the valley and keep an eye on the herds, as they were looking for a stray cow, or had to relieve themselves, or perform ablutions. They never prayed, of course, but this was one of their excuses for leaving Osko alone when they saw someone approaching the shrine. But it wasn't long before they no longer needed to justify their absences; they would grab the food and eat it, divide whatever was left, and then come back. Osko would pay them no heed, as he was sure to be distracted with something, and it never occurred to him to ask about where they went, or why it took them so long, or what they were carrying when they returned.

Osko's favourite pastime involved the bird they call the "shepherd's pleasure", or the nightjar, which would often fly in front of a shepherd as he was leading his herd, and then land nearby. The shepherd would then begin the game: he would throw stones at the bird, perhaps to shoot it down, but more to amuse himself and find some relief from his loneliness. The bird would keep the shepherd entertained, fooling him into thinking that he'd managed to bring it down, only to fly off at the last moment and come down another few steps ahead. In this way, the "shepherd's pleasure" took Osko far away from his flock; on his way back, he grew tired from having to gather animals that had almost completely scattered, and then he had to take a rest as he cursed his ill luck as a hunter, swearing that the damned bird wouldn't get a chance to escape next time.

At the same time, Ramko and Hawase's lot only got better and better. They no longer had to amuse themselves with hunting birds; instead, they benefited a great deal from their proximity to the shrine. The geography worked in their favour, as did their luck: their work forced them to keep close to the shrine, where pasture was abundant, and their luck led them to the offerings that had been left behind. As their game developed further, it became a very profitable pastime for such a remote mountain region. They would hide, or one of them would hide, from the visitors, then he would reappear in the guise of a servant of the shrine and take their lawful share.

"God's sustenance for a blind wolf." They'd repeat this saying, laughing, after every operation, and especially after the most profitable visits, like those from visitors who came from far away, outside the province of Mardin. These would leave particularly generous offerings at the shrine, as if trying to compensate for the rarity of their visits to the Holy Sheikh Latane, or to urge him to grant their wishes more quickly.

Chapter 22

Armed with prayers and supplications and many wishes of good fortune, Khatoune gathered her few possessions and put them in her bundle, which had accompanied her like her best friend for many years. She didn't want to talk about her son, whom she hadn't yet heard from or seen. She had been told that he'd been asked more than once about whether he might want to return home, where his mother was waiting for him. But he had always categorically refused, never wanting to discuss it. Whenever Khatoune thought about this, she was tortured by worry and misery the likes of which she'd never experienced before. Her life had been filled with disasters and tragedies, and while she'd always faced up to them, she could rely on the fact that they'd never leave her alone.

She refused to admit to herself that her heart had become overwhelmed with pain. This had happened to her before, but her vitality and strength and patience had worked to suppress it, and rather brought out its very opposite, her willpower and determination in the face of endless challenges. She was often, for this reason, talked about as if she were a man, or at least the equal of men. This was meant as high praise, for features that were fully deserving of it; but it both cheered and annoyed her. She liked that she was praised and respected, according to the prevailing social mores. But, on the other hand, she didn't see men as having any features that would make them intrinsically superior or different. Perhaps they thought it was the thing between their legs that made them so special. "But being a man," she'd say, "is only about being strong in the heart; it is nothing but courage, and it's not determined by outward appearance. It's not a matter of moustaches or beards." She was respected by everyone, and yet her words weren't taken seriously. They were more like a joke, and nobody thought more deeply about them.

Her intention was to perform her five daily prayers at Sheikh Latane's shrine. Every place brings a particular degree of merit, and that of a holy shrine is doubled, for supplications made in one are answered, and requests are fulfilled, by the will of the Almighty.

She informed her host that she intended to leave that night, after midnight. This didn't give Perishane much time to express her disapproval of what Khatoune was saying, and she soon gave up on it, not asking Khatoune to linger or stay longer. She knew her completely, and she knew she wouldn't be able to convince her to change her decision; for, if she'd been able to do that, she would have done so decades ago, when she had exhausted all the possible means at her disposal and still failed to make her stay. It seemed as if she were obeying orders that could not be questioned.

Perishane wiped a tear from her cheek, then went to prepare some provisions for Khatoune. She tried to send one of her children with her, but Khatoune obstinately refused.

"Have you forgotten, Perishane, that I'm a daughter of these mountains? How can you be worried that something would happen to me here?"

"There are beasts and wolves around . . . ."

"They'll fear me, and I won't be scared of them."

"Just wait until dawn, at least."

"Night and day are the same to me. And you know what it is I need to do."

A little after midnight, she woke up Hawar, kissed him on his forehead, and whispered in his ear:

"This is it, my child. And may God help us."

She urged him to kiss Perishane's hand, for he was to accompany her to the shrine, and after that to Qarashike, where she would find her son Ahme. Perhaps if she prayed in the Sheikh's presence, and made a sacrifice to his holy spirit, she might be able to convince her son, whom she knew very well. He was stubborn, like his mother, and nobody and nothing could change his mind, except perhaps the intervention of his Sheikh, or one of his successors, who might be able to convince him that doing a thing would mean obeying God's will, and the Sheikh's, and that it was a matter of fate and couldn't be avoided.

She thanked God for Perishane, who gave her two turkeys, slaughtered and plucked, so that Khatoune could present them as a sacrifice and offering to the spirit of the Sheikh. One turkey would be for her, and the other for Khatoune, and perhaps its blood and its meat—which would be offered as food for the hungry—would, by the power of God, serve to turn Ahme away from his fateful decision. For blood, when it is shed, can make trouble and misfortune disappear, and push out adversity. It can rise in the eyes of the envious and turn their deception back on them, and both quench and purify the lust for killing. She had to anoint her hand with blood and press it on what needed to be purged of grief and envy, wrapping it in a veil that would protect from jealous eyes; for, when the blood dried, it could engender feelings of awe and terror in whoever saw it and urge them into thinking and reflection, inspiring them to seek refuge with God from their misfortune, or shedding blood when it should not be shed.

Khatoune had decided to visit the sheikh even before she had left her house; yet still she'd waited a little, so she might hear what was being said about Ahme, and his decision about whether or not to come home.

She walked in the light of the moon, avoiding the rocks with well-practiced manoeuvring, talking to herself out loud without quite knowing why. The silence was oppressive, and the night was still, without a touch of a breeze. The calm lay heavy on the tension hidden in her heart. So she asked, even though she didn't expect Hawar could answer her:

"Do you think that he'll want to come back home?"

But what home would he return to? He was an exile everywhere he went. What home did she mean? He was a stranger, and the son of a stranger, in every village that he visited; he was hungry and poor and deprived, and the son of an old woman who could not speak about secrets she had promised never to reveal.

Her words were bitter from the length of the life that she had lived, and suffered, until life itself became nothing but suffering. (Home?) It was a choking agony, a painful memory that awakened sorrows in her and stirred them until they became a volcano that flared and flared and wouldn't erupt, a slow death that grew anew with every moment, and would give no respite - a death so unlike the death people knew, and which they described as an eternal rest.

What home, Khatoune?

The words came in a deep voice that shook her, making her tremble. It echoed all around, from the mountain summits to the fruits on the treebranches, all the way to the stars, the rocks, the bats and the birds, the soil and the herds in the pastures. She turned around, feeling like everything around her, the things she knew and the things she didn't know, was groaning and shouting and echoing with her words. Then she heard it again, with a different rhythm, and hoarsely, as if with pain:

What home, Khatoune?

Hawar, who was walking behind her, had never seen her like this before. He didn't know what had come over her, and what had stolen her away from him and the world around them. In the end, he just stood next to her. She wouldn't stop repeating the same words, over and over, words that she made sound like a curse:

What home, Khatoune?

He couldn't interrupt her. She was spinning around wildly, talking to everything and nothing at once. She looked light, if not weightless, as if gravity could no longer affect her. She raised her hands to the stars, talked softly to the moon, cradled the stones, waved her bundle and the turkeys in their bag. Hawar was too afraid to ask what had come over her; he was completely baffled, too confused to say anything. Then a single tear trickled from his eye, and he saw his grandmother shouting at the top of her voice: *What home, you idiot?*

Then she fell down to the ground and burst into a sobbing fit that lasted for a long time. She was oblivious to everything, even her Hawar, who was still standing by her side.

"I'm so worried about you, Mother."

The pain in his voice was sharp enough to break his grandmother's heart. She looked at him, silent, her face full of tears, but he didn't wait for her to respond:

"What did you mean when you said that? When you said 'what home, Khatoune?"

"Our home."

Her voice was faint and broken. She was perplexed by the state she was in; she could see from Hawar's panicked expression that something had happened that shouldn't have, and that he couldn't understand.

"What home do you mean?" he asked again, desperate for an answer. "Do you mean our house?"

"Come and follow me to the shrine. And no more questions."

It pained her to have to say it so sharply, but there was no other way to repel Hawar's persistent questioning. His thirst for knowledge couldn't be easily sated, and a simple answer wouldn't be enough.

"But you didn't tell me what home you were talking about. And why were you crying?"

He felt as though he had to comfort his grandmother somehow, and he wanted to know the real reason for her sudden strange behaviour.

"It's everywhere, we're at home everywhere. Now come, light of my life. We have to hurry."

She said this with her usual calm, and this finally reassured and comforted Hawar.

"To the grave, Mother?" he asked, a little more brightly.

"Yes, mother's dearest. To the shrine."

She sounded confident and determined, and Hawar was happy.

Chapter 23

Hawar followed his grandmother as she circled the shrine and performed her rites. He watched her pensively and in silence. He was struck by the awesome, terrifying nature of the place, and the feeling of holiness that overcame all visitors. This, perhaps, he let himself feel to a much greater extent. He wanted to interrupt his grandmother more than once, but always stopped himself; she looked deeply engrossed in her prayers and supplications. But his hunger prevailed in the end, and loosened his tongue, and he timidly asked for something to eat. Only then did his grandmother realise how oblivious her sobs and supplications had made her to everything around her. She sought refuge with God from the accursed Satan, and cursed him again for good measure, for Satan was the source of all trouble and evil. She was still praying under her breath as she took some bread and cheese and dates out of her bundle. She told Hawar to invoke God's name, and then to eat; the poor boy looked famished from his travails. He ate voraciously, like he never had before, and then stretched out and dozed off where he lay, with crumbs of bread still scattered all over his legs.

Everything around him was singing and talking to him: the birds who'd left their nests in search of food, chirping as if they were greeting him; the trees moistening the ground with dew; and the voices of the livestock in the distance, bleating and grumbling and mooing and braying; and occasionally the barking of the dogs that always accompanied the herds . . . all of it in a complex, rarely witnessed harmony.

When Hawar rose from his nap, he felt strangely reinvigorated. He drank some water, but didn't wash his face. He wanted to save it for drinking, for they had a long day ahead of them and they might otherwise run out. His grandmother had taken her place on a stone bench covered with some dried grass, with her back to the east. She looked calm, enveloped with hope and serenity, basking in the warmth of the sun's rays. She was facing the tomb, a small modification to the direction of her prayer.

Hawar's newfound vigour made him restless, and he could hardly just sit around and watch his grandmother, who in any case seemed oblivious to everything around her, praying to God and asking His forgiveness, through the Sheikh's intercession. So he set out to explore his surroundings. The many different sounds that he had heard surely meant there was a lot going on. He paced a few times across the small clearing around the shrine, where his grandmother could see him; he wanted to reassure her that he wouldn't go far. Then he started to poke his head behind the trees and rocks, and a long time passed before his innocent movements seemed to have reassured his grandmother; it would look as if he were pursuing a bird, or amusing himself by trying to catch a lizard, or fooling around with a hedgehog, or peeing, and soon he'd be moving freely among the trees. He'd step around a tree, and lean on it, and start to pee, and observe the little holes that his pee made in the ground. He was delighted by this, and especially so after sensing the heady smell of his pee, which smelled a little like the piss of a goat.

He began his explorations, and soon enough noticed the herds of cattle and sheep that were grazing toward the east, scattered through the valley and the pastures as far as the eye could see. Among them, he saw the smoke rising from a gathering of three shepherds who looked like they were getting ready for breakfast.

It was Ramko who noticed him first, a little startled that someone would be around so early. He called the boy over, beckoning him to come closer and join them. When Hawar didn't respond, he made his way over to him. At first, Hawar was frightened and suspicious, due to his grandmother's constant warnings, but Ramko managed to win some trust from him, and the boy felt a little more reassured when he invited him to join them for breakfast. Still, he approached them only slowly. But he managed to relax around them, and after they were introduced and they started joking with one another, it was as if he'd known them for a very long time. He said that he'd been at the shrine since dawn with his grandmother, and then told them as much as he could about her, and how she had come to visit the Sheikh so he would help her convince her son to return home with her, and to her, after he had left her to ask around after him to no avail.

Ramko had hardly been caught off guard before. But this, now, put him in a tight spot. How could he solve his problem, and especially given Hawar already knew he was a shepherd? There was nothing to it but to resort to what Ramko thought of as his cunning; this, he often used to outsmart both Osko and Hawase, and he had no lack of tricks he could employ. So he feigned modesty, and toned down his jokes, and wished good luck to Hawar and to his grandmother, then gave him a pan of warm milk to drink. He then told him that he was, in fact, the man in charge of the shrine, but he'd been late that morning, because he'd noticed a wolf trying to sneak into the valley.

He only concocted this excuse after he'd learned from Hawar that his grandmother was determined to stay until she'd finished her night prayer, and that she'd brought two turkeys as sacrifice and offering to the spirit of the Sheikh. Both Ramko and Hawase made it look as if they had understood Hawar's story completely, even though the names of places and people confused them. What they

| 151 |

were sure of, or more accurately what mattered to them most, was that Hawar's grandmother had brought meat that she was due to leave as an offering. Meanwhile, Osko hummed Turkish songs that he didn't know very well, and to which couldn't pronounce the words properly, and played with his flute, which he used as a stick as he didn't know how to play it.

Hawar didn't want to worry his grandmother by being gone for too long, as she might feel the need to pause her prayers and start looking for him, so he excused himself, saying that he needed to go back to the shrine. Ramko said he would go with him. He gave Hawase a wink, the meaning of which was clear to both, and which hinted at the joy he felt when he was on the cusp of getting his hands on particularly rich booty. Out loud, he only asked Hawase and Osko to keep an eye on the herds until he came back.

Upon approaching the tomb, Ramko cleared his throat. He'd been hitting his stick around, as if trying to clear small stones from the path. Now, he kept his eyes down, though he was focused entirely on the young boy's grandmother. He then swept together a few piles of twigs and thorns, which had accumulated around the Sheikh's tree. Everything there was named after the Sheikh, associated with him and made to be his own: the tree was the Sheikh's tree, and the rock was the Sheikh's rock, and the tomb was the Sheikh's tomb, the tree branches belonged to him, and so on. There was another grave close by, which was said to be the grave of his wife. Everything that was close to the shrine was his, and it was all given its due measure of respect, and anyone who desecrated it would have his guts burned from the inside out or suffer some other of the various woes that featured in the stories told among the locals.

Hawar told his grandmother that he'd met the servant of the

shrine. Ramko then came forward and greeted her, "Peace be upon you," in the proper Muslim manner. He introduced himself and told her that he'd heard about her and her story in the village, and also that he knew her son, Mulla Ahme Benxati, a man with a good and most pious reputation. He then plucked some appropriate folk sayings from his memory, about how good the Sheikh was to those who asked him for help, and how he visited them in their sleep, and gave them what they needed. And, of course, he didn't neglect to slip in that he was the one who received the offerings and donations to distribute them to the poor and needy, and to travellers passing through.

Khatoune liked Ramko's tales, and especially his praise of her son. The stories gave her hope - of how the spirit of the good Sheikh helped people in need and made their wishes come true.

As Ramko set out to resume his cleaning duties, Khatoune asked him to make sure that he distributed her offerings for the Sheikh's spirit, and also that Perishane had charged her to make a sacrifice on her behalf.

"And you?" Ramko asked. "What are you both going to eat?"

"God is generous. Don't worry about us."

"You said Perishane charged you with presenting her offering."

"She did."

"So then. It's your right to eat from it. And it's your right to feed your children from your own offering."

Ramko had now decided that he'd share one of the turkeys with them and hide the other to share it with Hawase. The old woman would stay at the shrine until the night prayer, which was far too long a time for him to stay hungry; of course, he wouldn't be able to steal the meat until after she left. So he tried to convince her that this was the right thing to do. He used all of his well-practiced cunning, honed through his many encounters with the visitors to the shrine whose offerings he'd stolen. Not a single one had doubted him in all the time he'd been helping himself to the offerings with his friend. He'd grown skilful in flattering the visitors, and pretending humility, and suggesting what should happen to the offerings. They would get confused, as they had never really thought about it; and, in the end, they conceded and let him dispose of them, trusting the honesty and compassion they saw in his eyes, and the good work he did in service of the shrine, and as a shepherd.

Khatoune was no exception. Like other visitors, she sympathised with Ramko and was misled by his apparent honesty. She liked his advice and was persuaded that it was sound.

"Then you can act on my behalf and Perishane's," she said. "And dispose of my sacrifice."

Chapter 24

Ahme finished his night prayer without any of the supplementary movements or supplications that he'd usually add, for he had a lot to do to prepare for his mother's visit. He'd had news that she would come, and he'd also heard that she would spend time at Latane's shrine. His heart was beset with doubt, rising and clamouring, fear and yearning and dread and longing all mixed together. He was a prisoner of his quarrelling emotions: the joy of reunion, the bitterness of the past, and the uncertainty of the future.

He didn't move away from the bench. He'd turn from one side to the other, then raise his hand to his forehead as if he were giving a salute. It was a determined, exaggerated motion, like it was meant to give him a power of special sight that would let his straining eyes penetrate the creeping darkness of the night. It seemed that nature here did a better job than any wonders of civilisation: many villagers were capable of clear sight even at night, perhaps because their eyes were well accustomed to darkness, and they could cheat it by using what little light there was to distinguish certain points and features in the landscape. And so Ahme caught sight of his mother, and Hawar, even as the shroud of night enveloped them. It was his mother, and with her, his dearest Hawar - who was Ahme's greatest weakness, especially after the death of his father Alo, who had been a father and a friend and a brother and everything else to Ahme, before the disaster that had split apart their souls before it did the same to their bodies.

His wife Sayre was hard at work, preparing dinner to welcome

Hawar and her mother-in-law. She would soon be calling her "Mother", as if trying to compensate for the motherly affection that she'd lost early in her life, when she'd lost her mother, and she would call Hawar her son, to show the tide of maternal feelings that had begun to come over her. She yearned for a child, and yet would never see one, so she found a son that looked like her husband. Their arrival completely changed the daily routine of Ahme's house, his wife trying to make up for lost motherhood twice over.

He saw them coming from far off. The darkness hardly affected him; the moon shone brightly, and the broadness of the plain gave the night particular shades and colours that could be easily distinguished.

He felt a shiver pass through his body; he didn't know why, and he couldn't express what was going on in his heart. He felt strangely light, as though the winds could pick him up and play with him. He wiped off his sweat, praising God and His strength and His greatness, and asking Him for forgiveness. The earth seemed to wobble under his feet, like a tremor was making him lose his balance. His hands felt heavy, and he didn't know what to do with them; maybe put them in his pockets, or let them drop to his sides, or wipe off more sweat with them, or rest them on his stomach as if he were getting ready to pray. The whole upper half of his body was swaying back and forth, like a madman obsessed with repeating the name of God, or a Sufi overcome by the ecstasy of love for his Master.

Khatoune was walking slowly, muttering her supplications, when Hawar stopped her:

"There's a big crowd just outside the village. Maybe they heard us coming?"

Men and women and children: nearly everyone from the village was there, with the mayor at their head. But Sufi Ahme still sat in his place next to the door of his house. He couldn't decide what to do. He called his wife, who asked him what he wanted, and then he changed his mind. He didn't know what he wanted anymore.

He didn't know how long it took her to approach him, whether minutes or hours, and she likewise didn't realise how she found herself face to face with him. He fell on his hands and knees before her, bowing and kissing and crying and apologising, while she responded with her own tears and prayers.

They wept in silence, and nobody knew how long it went on, as though time had stopped existing for them, all of them taking part in the same banquet of tears, tears of joy and sorrow all at once. So the villagers discovered something that they would never before had thought possible: the tears of reunion. For reunion could be a strange thing, and more difficult than parting or saying goodbye.

Khatoune spoke softly to her son Ahme, like a mother to a baby in the cradle. He'd submitted himself completely to her embrace. She swayed him gently, and patted his back, and he was on the verge of tears that he didn't know how to stop, other than waiting for them to pass.

The gathered crowd was stunned and amazed by what they saw. The coming of Khatoune to Qarashike was an exceptional event. It stirred everyone, making them think at once about themselves and their loved ones. It strengthened family ties and made people appreciate each other's presence in their lives.

It was a moving sight, even more so than the experience of parting.

Khatoune then turned to her daughter-in-law, who hurried to kiss her hand and take her share of the tears, which was plentiful, and Ahme turned to Hawar and hugged him for a long time. He kissed him all over, embracing him with all his affection, all the love and compassion and longing that he'd been holding on to for so long. It included his love for Alo, and for Hawar himself, who was after all the treasure that he wanted to preserve at whatever cost. Hawar, in turn, was still awe-struck by the turn of events. This was the first time he'd seen his grandmother so vulnerable, and also the first time in years that he'd seen his uncle Ahme, who had changed a lot. He was heavier now, and his beard had turned grey, and the clothes he wore made him look even older.

Hawar was the only person there who hadn't added a single tear to the flood of tears at the reunion, and he blamed himself for it. At first, he looked like a strange boy to his uncle: he'd grown taller and more mature, though his face was still that of a child.

It was a night unlike any other, and none of them were tempted by rest or sleep. They stayed up in Ahme's house long into the night. And even after the villagers had finished welcoming their guests and scattered to their homes, Khatoune stayed up with her son and his wife. They could have talked and talked, recounted countless misfortunes and worries, but Khatoune ignored all that, and rather blessed their marriage, and prayed for their good luck, and for the health of their children - even though she knew from the moment she saw her that Sayre would never give birth, as she was past her child-bearing years. Still, Khatoune wanted to comfort her, and prayed for her children even though she knew it was too late, and that her prayers would never be answered.

Ahme sat between Hawar and his mother, kissing his mother's hand and then Hawar's forehead in turn, while his wife untiringly fulfilled her duties as a host, making more and more tea as the hours passed.

There was time for everything... except for convincing Ahme to come back. He was unmovable, for he had destroyed everything that connected him to the past. He'd chosen his path, and he swore that he wouldn't swerve from it. He even tried the impossible, trying to talk his mother and Hawar into staying with him.

Chapter 25

Hawar visited Mardin twice and still wished he had more time to spend there. He loved the city, as it was stranger than all the other cities he'd ever visited or heard about. It gave him a special feeling that he couldn't define or explain.

On his first visit, he didn't know what to expect. But, as usual, he had an unmatched thirst for exploration, and he could have flown from happiness when his uncle Ahme told him that he would take him to Mardin the following morning. He almost didn't sleep at all as he drew fantasy maps of Mardin in his head. He'd heard so many stories about it! The one that caught in his memory was a strange tale he'd heard from his grandmother about a man in Mardin Prison, which stood at the top of the mountain in the centre of the city, around which buildings had spread, and which gave the city its distinctive shape. The prisoner escaped by some very strange means: it was said that God himself provided a gust of wind that carried him up from the prison courtyard and deposited him far away, on the other side of the border. This saved him from the horrors that he had been suffering, and the noose that was due to be tightened around his neck in a few days' time. The miracle more than proved his innocence. His robe served as a parachute that helped him fly along and across the border. Indeed, he was innocent; it was the chief guard in his village - Qasre - that had accused him of helping the rebels, because he'd refused to give him a sheep to roast when he was drunk on duty. So the chief guard from the village of Zaydiyye visited him, accusing him of smuggling weapons across the border and looting the guard post, something that had happened a couple of years earlier, though the culprit had never been found.

After these events, the prisoner became a saint of God. His fame grew, spreading far and wide. But as he was a true saint hidden in the form of a simple man, he died soon after his secret was discovered, for he had asked God to take him before he could become vain.

Apart from this story, Hawar's mind also conjured a number of images that formed his idea of Mardin: tall staircases, houses that were carved into the mountainside, and a wealth of treasures beneath it, hidden in the depths of the mountain. He remembered some of the story of Princess Marya, who betrayed her father and came to a secret agreement with a warlord who then attacked and occupied her city. But the warlord captured her and tied her hair to the tail of his horse, dragging her behind him through the streets of Mardin and then leaving her corpse to be plundered by his soldiers. "One who betrays her father and her family," he said, "will not hesitate to betray anyone."

The full story tells us that there was a king against whom no place or city had ever rebelled, whom no one had ever opposed. He conquered Mardin, but its castle defied him. His army camped next to it, and he then tried to send his followers into the castle. Thus he learned that the ruler of the fortress had a daughter called Marya, who was young and beautiful, but also ambitious. So he sent her messages expressing his love for her and that he wanted to marry her, and that he'd crown her queen over all the lands that were under his rule. Her grand ambition spurred her into betrayal: she revealed to him one of the secret entrances into the castle, and so handed the city over to the king, before she would hand over herself . . . and tragedy ensued. A different story gives Marya the mantle of holiness: she was the saint whose name became associated with the city - or perhaps it was the city that became associated with her name.

Hawar followed his uncle's advice and made sure to follow closely behind him, and to lean against the walls so that his feet wouldn't slip. The roads were paved with stones, and the stairs showed no mercy to the clumsy or the reckless. They headed to Sheikh Jamil's shop, which was in the Grocers' Market: to reach it, you had to descend fifty steps from the main road, then turn left into a narrow alley, walking on for more than fifty metres; and there, somewhere among the shops under archways carved into the rock - among the butchers with their meat, and the sellers of vegetables and groceries - sat Sheikh Jamil, who could trace his descent back to a long line of other sheikhs. He wore a green cap and a very clean robe, and he held a long misbaha of green prayer beads. He looked almost like he'd been expecting them; he welcomed them warmly and exchanged kisses with Ahme, then kissed Hawar as well. "Surely this is Hawar," he said to Ahme, "who you're always telling me about!"

He gave them some water, then accepted the yoghurt and eggs that Ahme had brought with him. He then gave him back his empty containers, and some dry goods like tea and sugar and rice, as well as some money - both as change, and for what he would bring him next time.

Hawar noticed that his uncle was very relaxed around Sheikh Jamil. He broached a subject he usually never did: his life and work when he was in Amouda, before he'd settled in Qarashike. He talked about it at length after Sheikh Jamil asked him about Amouda, and about some of his relatives there. Hawar then felt comfortable enough to ask the Sheikh about the meaning of the name of Mardin, and how far back it went in history; he'd already asked his uncle about it, but Ahme's answers hardly sated his thirst for knowledge.

"In the past, this was a Syriac city," Sheikh Jamil replied. "And Mardin comes from a Syriac word, which meant 'fortress'. They say that, in Aramaic, it means the same thing. But the Christians are a minority here now. Most of the people living here today are Arabs and Kurds and Turks; though there are some Christians as well. And even though they've been declining, they still support and care for the two oldest monasteries in the world, both of which are close to here, the monasteries of Mar Hananiya and Mar Gabriel.

"As for us," the Sheikh went on, regretfully, "the Muslims, well, we care about nothing other than fighting each other. See, when the Christians were in charge, they were all traders and jewellers. But we've ignored the mosques and forgotten our religion. And our faith and our lives are a lost cause for God."

Hawar would later be able to add to this information what he read about Mardin in books: for example, that it was built on the top of a mountain that reached 1100 metres in height, with a well-fortified castle at its very top, reached by the narrowest of paths. Writers called it the Queen of Castles, noting that it was an important defensive point that was often besieged. It came under Persian rule in 226 AD. The Persians fortified it, using its hills and heights to create a powerful stronghold to fight off their enemies, the Byzantines. It then came under Byzantine rule, until it was returned to the Persians in 363 AD, under a peace treaty signed between Jovian and Shapur the Great. The Persians and the Byzantines then alternated in ruling Mardin until it was conquered by the Arabs under Iyad ibn Ghanm in 640 AD.

The Arabs seemed to believe the name of the city was derived from words for rebellion and insubordination. Yaqut al-Hamawi's medieval book on geography, the *Mu'jam al-Buldan* or the *Encyclopedia of*

Countries, tells us the following: "*Mardin* should have an *i* between the *r* and the *d,* so that in fact it looks like the plural of *marid,* or a rebel. I believe this is because whoever came up with this name heard that Queen Zenobia had said: 'Marid rebelled and al-Ablaq withstood.' And when they saw the marvellous fortifications of this castle, they said: 'These here are many rebels, not just one *Marid.*' Mardin is a castle on the top of a mountain above the Mesopotamian plain. It looks out on Dara and Nisibin and Dunaysar and all that wide area, and it is surrounded by vast areas of housing which include markets, inns, schools, hospices, and shrines for the Sufis. The houses are stacked like staircases, one house on top of another. Every street looks out on the houses below, and there is a clear view of the plain from each of the roofs. They have few wells for water, and they mostly drink from cisterns that have been set up in their houses. Surely there is no finer castle anywhere in the world, and none better fortified."

After they had rested and drank their tea with Sheikh Jamil, Hawar's uncle took him around the shops, to get him a few presents. There were now echoes in uncle Ahme of that young man who would joke and sing throughout the night: he moved smoothly, with a lightness and happiness that he'd thought he had lost forever. Hawar followed him, delighted. He would walk behind him and talk to him about the beauty of Mardin and the kindness of its people, even though he didn't know anyone there apart from Sheikh Jamil.

Ahme bought him local delicacies, roasted nuts and chickpeas, and sweet sheets of apricot and grape leather that they called *bastik* and *'uqud,* as well as three kilograms of courgette seeds, which were smooth and not very salty and tastier than pumpkin seeds. He then asked him whether there was anything else that he wanted or needed, in a friendly manner that he hadn't adopted before. Hawar didn't ask for anything, but his uncle insisted he should choose what he wanted.

So he picked out a carved brooch with the portrait of a woman who was said to have been a queen. Though he didn't know the woman's name, he was excited to have found it, and the brooch accompanied him for many more years, until it got stolen one day on a crowded bus. He mourned it for several months, and he never forgot it. Its loss pained him forever.

They had to be at the bus stop before noon, as the only minibus departed around twelve o'clock, and it wouldn't wait for anyone. Hawar hadn't had nearly enough of Mardin; he was desperate to see the entire city, from its first stone to the last, even those hidden deep in the ground.

The glorious picture of Mardin that he'd painted in his head had all but evaporated, for he'd now seen its market bursting with vegetables and fruit and cheese and dairy, and the skins of sheep and goats hanging outside the butchers' shops, as well as a few other streets that looked no cleaner than those in the market. But the images he'd conjured still stayed in his imagination, and in his dreams, and he decided he had to come back to explore the city and its many quarters.

"Is this still Mardin, Uncle?" he asked innocently. "And why are there so many statues here of that guy as well?"

"This is old Mardin, my son. The new Mardin is being built now, and new buildings rise up every day. It's behind that hill." Ahme pointed toward the northwest of the city. "And, as for the statues, it's not the same guy as you have over there! It's someone else."

"But he looks just like him, Uncle! And his statues are everywhere as well."

Ahme had no response to that.

"Have you been to the new Mardin, Uncle?"

"I haven't, no. I've got no business there."

Hawar was surprised that his uncle hadn't seen all of Mardin, and only knew a street or two, and a couple of shops that he frequented for his supplies, without ever thinking to explore the rest of the city. Hawar decided he would have to explore it when he next visited—*if* he visited again. So he asked his uncle:

"Do you promise we can walk around and explore Mardin together next time we're here, Uncle?"

"I promise, my son."

He said it automatically, just to quell Hawar's enthusiasm, certain that he'd forget about it in a few days' time.

Chapter 26

As for Hawar's second journey to Mardin:

It was at Eid, when the Turkish and Syrian governments had agreed that they would let families visit each other across the border, but for no more than 48 hours. Hawar was happy because his uncle did not deny him his visit to Mardin; he would take yoghurt and eggs and bring back some domestic supplies, as well as presents his wife had asked for, for his nephew. He was, moreover, bound by the promise he'd made, and which Hawar hadn't forgotten.

It was a cold, still winter morning. Steam rose from the ground as it was slowly warmed by the sun, and smoke rose from the ovens and stoves of the village, congealing into small clouds that would never bring rain, however much people might pray for it. Dogs' barking echoed between the buildings. The turkeys huddled in corners; the chickens had taken refuge in their coops; in the cattle pens, the cows yawned lazily. The rays of the sun had illuminated some of the higher roofs, and sparrows had begun to flutter from one roof to another. To head to Mardin, you had to get up at dawn: the holidays were ending, and the students had to get back to their schools in the city.

The minibus from Dare was supposed to come at six. Hawar got up quite a bit earlier, to get ready for his journey, and found his uncle sitting on his prayer rug, fully dressed, having already called the dawn prayer and prayed both the obligatory prayer and the sunna. He prayed for mercy for his mother and his ancestors, he prayed for heaven for himself and for his wife, and he prayed for his nephew so he would have faith and luck in his life. As Hawar waited for him to finish, he saw that fresh bread had already been put out for breakfast. This surprised him, on such an early morning, and especially that winter morning, when he thought about all the stages that bread had to go through: kneading and proofing and firing up the oven and baking it until brown. It was women who took on this task - as they took on many others - of putting out all the different foods on the table. In these lands, it was always women who were the last to go to sleep and first to rise, the last to eat and the first to slaughter, as if they were the natural-born leaders of the people. The women's daily toil was surely a form of resistance, and their ultimate cause; and their first concern was to educate their children so they wouldn't repeat the mistakes of their parents, and their ancestors. The advice they gave their children, along with their husbands, was spontaneous and sincere:

"We don't want you to live a life like ours."

"We don't want you to suffer what we have suffered, and still do."

"We want you to achieve what others before you have failed to do."

"We've lived in want and misery, and we'll give our lives so you won't have to do the same."

The minibus was late, as usual. The driver knew that the passengers would have to wait regardless; it wasn't as if they had much of a choice.

The minibus stopped in several villages on the way, carrying passengers and their luggage, as well as a large quantity of dairy products. The passengers were closely crammed together, but nobody complained; it was nothing unusual, especially because this time the bus was filled with students, who in addition to their bags were bringing books and other supplies, churns full of yoghurt and baskets full of eggs for the shops that they worked with, which they would use to pay their school fees and thus become a slightly more civilised type of villager.

The road wound its way through many curves and bends to reach the hilltop city, built where it could repel those who coveted it; the city of many tongues, whose inhabitants differed so much in their way of thinking from the people of the western provinces, as they did from those of the east; the city whose people certainly spoke Arabic, and of course Kurdish, and Turkish by necessity, and might also speak Aramaic, or Armenian, or even other languages, according to the occasion and the need.

Snow was falling all around - on the tops of the mountains, and down the slopes on to the roads. The icy temperatures froze it solid, making it look as though it would stay there forever. A light wind was blowing, but it was so cold it pierced through to the bones and made the travellers' noses sniffle, for good measure, and run.

Even though they stopped every hundred metres or less, none of the passengers complained; it seemed that they were used to it. Whenever the minibus stopped, all the doors would open: the driver would step out through the driver's door, then open the back door to get the luggage out; the passenger door would be opened so that passengers could get off with their things; and sometimes the driver would have to get up on the roof and take down some of the baggage that had been tied up there with rope, very tightly and securely given the winding and climbing roads. Everyone else just had to wait. When the driver finished, he'd dust off his clothes and get back to work. He didn't grumble or complain, unlike the drivers on most of the other routes; he knew the particular nature of the area, and apart from that most of the passengers were either his relatives or acquaintances.

They sat down in a coffeeshop in Mardin and drank tea, and Hawar was very grateful for the warmth inside the shop. A group of old men had gathered around the wood burner, but the old men paid them no heed, as they were preoccupied with their own discussion, a spontaneous exchange of views to which everyone brought their own personal opinion. The fundamental question was whether it was permissible to look around during prayer or not. They were talking in the Mardin dialect, which interposed Arabic words with Kurdish and Turkish, and voices rose and fell that supported the idea or opposed it.

Hawar asked his uncle what he thought about it, even though he already knew. Ahme didn't give an answer, and only said:

"God preserve us from idle chatter."

He didn't even consider discussing it further; the matter, for him, was settled. He would keep to Teacher's advice, which told him strictly not to discuss religion or politics with anyone, for to do so would only cause headaches. The other side could never be convinced, and the argument would only intensify as the participants became more stubborn and obstinate.

So they left the patrons and their chosen subject of the hour, and they headed out into the streets, empty but for students heading to school and people heading to work. It was not exactly the best time to play tourist, but the opportunity had to be seized. And, despite the difficulties in moving around, Hawar was intent on visiting a few of the historical sites that he'd heard about or seen on television. The main difficulty was climbing the stairs, which had turned into slopes of black ice. On a frosty morning, wandering around a city like Mardin was an adventure that could equally be met with success or failure, and there was no other choice but to plunge in and hope for the best, trying to get as much out of it as possible.

His uncle told him a proverb that was apparently widely shared among the Turks:

"Nobody can climb the steps of Mardin, other than the donkeys of Mardin!"

This is because, in the city, donkeys were used to transport goods, and they always knew their way and never strayed from it. This drove the Turks to make fun of the people of Mardin by talking about them in this way, with some wickedness and double entendre: the proverb could be read as saying that nobody can ever get used to scaling the staircases of Mardin other than Mardin's donkeys, or it might mean that the people of Mardin were themselves donkeys. In any case, it was always said with a smile and a wink to any of those mentioned who were present, to ward off any potential accusations of slander or ill intent.

Some of the sites that they managed to visit weren't in any better state than the ruins of Dare. They had obviously been looked after, given the city's status as the capital of the province, though they still hadn't been taken care of as well as they should have been. Hawar tried to look out toward Amouda, as he'd looked out from Amouda to Mardin, especially at night when the lights illuminated the flank of the mountain, strung out like a necklace placed to lure you toward it, kiss it, possess it, and enjoy its presence. But now, the fog lay thick, and there was almost no visibility. He felt sorry for Mardin and the plains below; he imagined how they might talk to each other, Mardin and the Mesopotamian plain; they would exchange blame and lament the pain of their separation. So he tried to give them hope and let hope sweep away the pain. The calls for reunion rose until they exploded in a silent scream: it blew apart the border posts and cut the electric fence that imposed frontiers upon the innocent, with murderous intent.

He broke off his line of thought, which would have spoiled anyone's fun. His vision didn't frustrate him, as it was not too far from the truth - the truth that remained, in its way, beautiful, despite the ugliness of the world. He saw it as a way to strip away the history, to break the pens of those who wrote it, and to give the brothers and sisters who'd been separated the means to cut through the fences and sweep away the mines so they would explode in the faces of those who'd planted them, cutting off the hands of those who'd played with maps and borders, which had changed innumerable times.

His feelings, though conflicted, did not disappear in Mardin. His thoughts stayed with him, and would not leave him - as if there was something that he still had to do there, a voice that still called for him, and urged him to return.

Chapter 27

Khatoune could not change her son's mind about coming back; nor could her son change her mind about staying. None of the arguments he put forward would convince her - not even when he promised that he would bring Shekrawka over to live with them, so they could live as one single family once more, after the disasters that had separated them. Khatoune had grown attached to her house and her town, where everyone knew her, yet knew nothing more about her than what they had seen with their own eyes. She also had doubts that she couldn't quite explain, but these did not go past the stage of vague suspicions, and so she prevaricated, trying to make herself forget them.

Ahme's stubbornness came directly from his mother. How else to explain their determination to convince the other that they were right? Hawar would tell himself this when he thought about their desperate conversations, which never asked what *he* might think about it, as if the matter didn't concern him at all.

After dawn prayer, Khatoune tied up her bundle and surprised Hawar by telling him they were leaving, even before she'd spoken to her son and daughter-in-law. They found no words to respond to this; their hopes had been shattered, and all their efforts and wishes had come to naught. Sayre had longed for her mother-in-law to stay, as she saw her like a mother to her, and perhaps she knew some remedies that might help make her pregnant . . . or some other means to fulfil her dream, given her experience as a child-bearer. She was now certain that she would never sieve the red soil to extract the pure, soft powder to sprinkle on the body of her child. And Ahme had likewise hoped that his mother and Hawar would stay, as he had only spent a few days with them, and felt that he had failed in his duty as provider for the needs of his family.

And while Khatoune had known beforehand that Ahme would not return to her, she had ignored that fact. Still, her hopes were in vain. She now recalled the nightmare that she'd tried to forget when there was first talk of her son's disappearance, and how she had honestly thought that he'd gone away "for the salt", as people said. Many myths and secrets revolved around this kind of voyage, but in short, it was believed that there was salt in abundance in some remote area in the east, and a family's breadwinner might go away with a caravan to return with the salt that would secure his family's livelihood. It was a long and arduous journey, and it cost the lives of many men. Another way to describe it was as "a trip with no return." This basically summed up what people thought when they'd lost all hope that a man would come home: he'd "gone for the salt", or on a journey for salt. This specific saying also referred to the roles and responsibilities of the provider for the family: he was obliged to secure the household's essentials, or in other words its salt.

Hawar had also hoped, in vain, that he could stay with both his grandmother and his uncle, together. His heart was split between them.

Khatoune didn't want to say goodbye to any of the villagers. She had only the utmost respect for the mayor and his family, but she'd already decided to leave in silence, unlike the huge commotion that had awaited her when she arrived, and which she also hadn't asked for. Misfortune followed her everywhere, but she did not want to talk much about this. People were victims of their own curiosity, and indeed could not be otherwise - she'd grown used to their attempts to pry and snoop and meddle in her affairs. She also refused her son's plea to accompany her to the border, as she wanted to suffer on her own. This formed her last line of attack against her son's defences, one that she always reliably employed, a reality that could be depended upon, and could not be brushed aside or ignored.

She broke her promise to Perishane and did not return to Dare. She headed straight for Amouda. When she approached the road that led to Nusaybin, Hawar noticed that his grandmother was trying to cross the highway at a place where there was a minefield on the other side, followed immediately by border posts. He tried to alert her to the grave danger that she would be exposing them to, but she paid him no heed. She said nothing, and instead kept walking in front. She knew the lay of the land much better than he did, and she had tested the borders before; she would tell the border guard that she'd been visiting her son, and she was only now returning to her home on the other side of the fence. She told herself that she might bribe the guard if he proved uncooperative, like other soldiers she recalled from the border whose cooperation could be easily bought, or who were in league with the smugglers.

Hawar froze in place. He didn't like his grandmother's blind charge ahead. He tried to draw her back toward the road, complaining that he was tired. But, unsurprisingly, his attempt met with failure. He had never seen his grandmother so oblivious to his pleas. When he realised she really wasn't listening, and that he'd fallen more than a hundred metres behind her, he ran after her, perhaps to grab her hand and forcibly drag her back. He found her behaviour reckless and foolish. Surely despair had overcome her, and she just wanted to rush back to her house, and the death that awaited her there, to spend the rest of her days with her grandson.

At that moment, the border guard heard the noise of their approach. He was suspicious about the old woman walking towards him with the bundle on her back; he couldn't know what was in it and suspected the worst. So he followed his orders to the letter. He called on her to stop and retreat, but she only waved her hand and tried to tell him something... and did not respond to his warning. He loaded his assault rifle and aimed it straight at her, to intimidate her and warn her against coming any closer. But she was intent on crossing her border, with her grandson in tow, as she had previously crossed it so easily with both of her sons, in the very same spot, without having to explain or justify herself. She spoke to the guard in Kurdish, telling him her reason for travelling, and he spoke back in Turkish, barking out his warning again and again. And before Hawar could reach her, he heard the shot ring out, silencing everything. His grandmother fell before his eyes. He ran to her, and the guard hurried to shoot at him as well, aiming perhaps to scare or hobble him, rather than to kill.

Chapter 28

With a calm that did not become her, and didn't become the blood gushing from her body, she strove to tell Hawar what he needed to know. She didn't want to imagine how they would react, Ahme, and Sayre, and Perishane and Pasho and all the other villagers that she loved and who loved her, when news reached them that she'd been killed. Rather, she focused all her strength on one thing: what she needed to tell Hawar.

"My dear Hawar, love of my heart . . . I remember you asked me what I meant when I said, 'What home, Khatoune?'"

She gave him no time to respond or consider. She went on, with a calm that was very odd in her situation; a real miracle, one could say, given the state of her wounded, bleeding body.

"Your grandfather was one of the rebels whose hopes were shattered before the revolt was brought down. They had high hopes and little means. They didn't do what they would've needed to do in order to realise their dreams. They were honourable and principled men, faced with a foe who had no mercy. Perhaps that's what broke their ranks, and extinguished their revolt.

"After it all ended, he stayed in hiding for a few months. The punitive expeditions during that time cost many lives, destroying everything in their path. A general amnesty followed, and he was one of those who were pardoned. But he was still to be drafted for military service. When he returned home, he'd decided to try and rebuild what had been destroyed, and return life to his land. In the first year of his marriage, he hadn't been able to enjoy the company of his bride, as he'd spent most of the time in the mountains with the rebels. He didn't witness the birth of his firstborn son, but only saw him later. I was left alone with his bride, to help and console her. The only thing that kept us going were his secret visits in the night, when he'd tell us stories about what the rebels would accomplish.

"But he couldn't fulfil his dreams, not even the smaller ones he had after he returned. They couldn't allow it. They couldn't just let him live his life, with his family and his children, on his land and in his village. They called him up for the army, even though his wife begged them not to take him, and I begged them at least to wait until the end of the harvest.

"He wasn't a chief or a sheikh or a mullah or a king. He thought they were all opportunists, working against the interests of their people. He revered only his sheikh, whom he saw as the ideal, because he wasn't like those who always searched for privileges and profits. Yes, Hawar. God rest him, he was the best possible father, and the best brother. He was one of the few who had learned to read and write. His wife was his sheikh's niece, and she was like a sister to me. We never fought. She treated me like a sister, and left no room for any doubt to come between us. She never made demands, and she would always ask my opinion when she wanted to do something. She might say, what do you think, Khatoune, if we feed the animals? My son! I swear, I've never met anyone like her, or anyone who would even come close to her virtue."

She drew a deep breath and looked straight into Hawar's eyes. He was anxious to learn everything, and his face implored her to continue, to tell him the story for which he'd waited for so long, and his father and his uncle before him, though they had never heard it and knew nothing about it.

Khatoune gasped so deeply that all her limbs trembled, and she closed her eyes.

Was she really dead? Would she leave him an orphan?

Hawar was on the verge of crying out in despair, like a sheep being led to slaughter. He couldn't sort out his feelings: whether he felt more sorrow for his grandmother, or for the story that she'd told him. Then he restrained himself when he saw that his grandmother had opened her eyes once again. It was as if she had postponed her death until she'd finished telling the tale that needed to be told. She had no time to ask Hawar about his growing anguish, whether it related to her or to the story of his grandparents that he'd otherwise never get to hear: about who they were, and about why they became homeless. These were a few big whys, that she had to try to explain to him.

"Yes, my son. There were four of us. Your grandfather, your grandmother, your father, and me. We didn't see your grandfather after he'd gone to the army—not until seven months later, when he came back for a short period of leave. It was a terrible parting, as we thought we'd never see him again. Yet we couldn't say that to each other. And the fear drove us apart.

"He was among those that Turkey sent out to the war in Korea, to fight the infidels. They were the enemies of Islam—or that's what they told us."

Hawar would not learn until later that Turkey, along with fifteen other countries, participated in the Korean War between 1950 and 1953, and sent many soldiers to the Far East in order to battle the Korean insurgents. This was before Turkey joined NATO, but doing

| 181 |

so helped its case for joining the alliance, proving its willingness and sincerity and loyalty to the anti-communist cause. It was almost like a third World War, and one of the bloodiest conflicts in history. It broke out soon after the end of the Second World War, when forces from North Korea, which was ruled by communists, invaded South Korea, which the Americans had recently withdrawn from. The United Nations considered the war a danger to world peace and demanded the communists withdraw; the member countries decided to help South Korea by granting it military aid. Sixteen countries did so, and they fought against the communists, as well as China and the Soviet Union, who supported them. The war ended with a ceasefire, but without any longer-term peace treaty. And one of its consequences was the death and displacement of millions on all sides that were party to the conflict.

"Your grandfather proved his courage there. He captured six Korean soldiers and led them bound to his commanding officer, together with all their equipment. The officer then asked his superiors to reward him for this heroic deed, which boosted morale and spread courage in the hearts of the other soldiers, who'd been exhausted by their longing for home and the strain of their duty, which left them wavering between two fires . . . both of them deadly.

"A year and more passed, and we were afraid to speak to each other about the fears that we felt so deeply. We heard many stories of the war, of killing and death, of people fleeing. Not everyone was affected by these tragedies, but they brought nothing but pain and suffering. Then your grandfather came back. His return was like a dream, a dream that many would never see fulfilled. Thousands were lost there, vanishing without a trace.

"His return brought up some terrible envy, and many rumours.

These were rumours about the money and riches and treasures that he had brought back. It was all so exaggerated. Everyone would add some new detail to the story, and it would grow and grow, with whatever people wanted to add to it. Your grandfather was the focus of many dreams and delusions, at a time when people were dying of hunger and poverty. And the evil eyes devoured him. Envy and hatred blinded people, turning their hearts against him. Envy and hate made them the most dreadful enemies, who could not be talked or reasoned with.

"So I ran off, with your father and your uncle, who was born while his father was away. They had been sleeping in my arms that night, when I put them down in the small room next to the well, away from your grandparents' room. I wanted your grandparents to enjoy their nights together, and perhaps to bring some joy back into their lives, to make up for their long separation that they'd had to suffer almost since they'd been married.

"I heard nothing but a loud scream, and then the shots. I got up. I was terrified. I made sure your father and uncle were well. I tried to get out and see what was going on. There was a fire in your grandmother's bedroom. A gang of thugs in masks wanted to steal your grandfather's money and all of his treasures that people had spun tales about . . . It was as if he'd brought back all of Korea with him. And the evil minds and jealous thoughts made sure to fill in the gaps.

"They murdered him and his wife. Yes. They murdered him. They burnt the house down, after they took all that they could find. None of the villagers would lift a finger to help us. Even though they were going to destroy everything and anything that we had.

"For a few days after, I felt I could die, for the one most dear to me was gone. I flooded her grave with my tears, every single day. I couldn't stay in that village, where it felt like all the villagers had conspired against us. I was afraid the thugs would come back and kill the two children that I'd managed to hide from them. I felt they would want to obliterate your grandfather's bloodline, so that nobody could claim his money and his property, and his blood.

"And on that dark night, I carried my brother's children, who would from then on be my children, for the rest of my life and theirs. And I fled. I didn't stop for two days. I swore I'd devote the rest of my life to them. I went through every village in Jayaye Omriyan. They called me Khatoune of Jayaye. And the kids were Alo and Ahme.

"I didn't want to be Khatoune, and I didn't want the children to be what they'd become.

"I'm your father's aunt, Hawar."

"You're his mother and his father. And you're my mother and my father too." Tears streamed down Hawar's face. He wanted to finish comforting his grandmother, and himself, but the tears had blocked his eyes. He wiped them off and saw that his grandmother was gone. Gone, never to return. She'd left him to his fate, by himself. All alone in the world.

"Mother, Mother . . . please."

His cry burst out, deep from his grief-stricken soul, his bleeding heart. But Khatoune, who had always done everything for him, could hear him no longer. She was back with his grandparents now, where she wanted to be.

A belated dedication

Dedicated, always, to those who seek to dissolve borders. Those who rebel against injustice, and those who help destroy maps. Those who erase the lines of latitude and longitude, so they might get the atlas they deserve, stripping away history and its crimes before the persistence of the land, despite the never-ending attempts to betray it, and empty it of its people.

The land, betrayed by history, is pushed to destroy itself, and collapse, and thus dissolve a person's belonging to it, to break them apart and force them to waver and fumble among its fragments, turned into a labyrinth where they might search in vain for a path to salvation. A path accompanied by hostility, where they might live at best the illusion of a life. This is the terrible image that any foe or oppressor wants their opponents to see, as it matches the description that he is looking for, and he might risk his life in order to preserve it.

A novel about the wretched geography of this land thus occupies a very special place. Its marginalisation does not erase its historical importance; and, by contrast to the logic applied by the enemy, its erasure does not mean that it is forgotten. The challenge is to remember those who would want to be forgotten, or pretend to be forgotten, and to remind others that they exist. Memory is the thing most worthy of trust, when trust is hard to find, for it does not betray those who do not betray it, and it does not deprive them of its presence. It helps whoever seeks refuge in it, and it hides whatever they think they will not need.

Memory is like the Preserved Tablet of predestination, which leads a person all the way to the origin of things and does not let them stand in awe before hollow spectacles. Memory is what a person needs most in their land, or in any other land they might end up living in. Memory is a weapon; it is the sacred bond; it is the code of honour that binds us to history. It is all a person can count on to preserve themselves, and their past, and their future.

It is not a matter of auctions in the town square or blind gambles. It is wanderings across the border; it is standing tall before a deadly electric fence. Scattered mental paradoxes, the urge for a single belonging and a renunciation of the pull of contradictory identities. Cries of refusal that concern everyone, every miserable person who rejects the tragic world torn apart by stolen oaths and worn-out alliances. And who, at the same time, calls to find the outlines of a world that was real before it was ever imagined.

Should we be able to cross the threshold of the border, which includes borders and landmines and scaffolds with all of their meanings, we would then enter into a conflict regarding equality of opportunity. Fought out in the arena of history, on a land that the past defends through its close connection with it, and through those who take refuge there, and through its excessive generosity, the refugees might think that they had settled in a land that was theirs anyway. They would persist in this, and they would persist with those who were generous to them. They would try to change it, seeking to replace the newcomers who had arrived after it had been emptied of those who had given it away, and granted them their residence and name and leave to stay . . . until their gratitude got turned into its very opposite. Thus, they would seek to treat wickedness by hurting another, and respond to friendliness and generosity with malice and vengefulness.

So the assault continues on this poor body that had come to fight against itself, and suffer many trials and tribulations, in the hope that it would soon wake up from its enforced slumber. Its hope in this, its saviour, is the modern world, which might finally destroy the old, sick tyrant that rules over it.

And as we wait for this salvation, we dream, and challenge, and grow firm.

Borders imprison hearts and minds. They cut off the blood and break the heart in two. They impose this on both sides, with no consideration for the people who have been cut off from their roots and forced to live their lives split apart, with severed limbs and severed emotions, blinded and confused, denied their true existence. Borders separate, oppressing the people of the border, on one side and the other, until they squeeze out all their hopes and become the burial ground for all who tried to cross and overcome them without agreement from the other side, and a barrier to any possible reconnection.

Such are borders. They hinder, and they bury.

Amouda, Syria, April 2009